INS MAN
Philco : a novel
Ken Mansfield.
30085000294871 $31.00
July 2018

DATE DUE

ADVANCE PRAISE FOR *Philco*

"If there was ever a ranking of 'Top 100 Most Interesting Lives in History,' Ken Mansfield would be on it. In *Philco*, he brings his experience and imagination to bear for you. This is a story that will stay with you forever."

—Andy Andrews, *New York Times* bestselling author of
The Traveler's Gift and *The Noticer*

"Reading a book by Ken Mansfield is always an adventure. Like any adventure, you never know where it's going to take you, or where you're going to end up. The one thing you do know is that it's going to be good. Now I have to go through that peculiar 'withdrawal' that I experience every time I finish a great book. I highly recommend *Philco*!"

—Kerry Livgren, founder, lead guitarist, songwriter of Kansas
"Dust in the Wind" and "Carry on Wayward Son"

"*Philco* is a very original work by one of the most original minds I know: Ken Mansfield. He is one of my favorite American writers and no one is better equipped to write about the subject matter at hand—a great country that lost its identity when God was asked to leave. It is a world that existed for Mansfield as a boy growing up alongside the Nez Perce Indian reservations in northern Idaho, and now, luckily for readers, those days live again in this special book."

—Marshall Terrill, author and executive producer *Steve McQueen: The Life and Legend of an American Icon*

"Today's times are constantly being redefined by the impact of culture under the auspices of technology, progress, and political correctness. *Philco* is a powerful journey back in time to what once was, and maybe, what could come to be, if we only learn to dream again. Ken Mansfield is the dreamer and *Philco* is the path to that dream…and deep down inside we all just want to get back to that place in our heart called home. Bravo, Ken!"

—Frank Sontag, host of *The Frank Sontag Show* 99.5 FM KKLA,
Los Angeles (Salem Media)

"*Philco* is a dream-like memory of an earlier, gentler America when the days of 'In God We Trust' echoed through time and eternity. Intriguing characters take Philco on a journey that causes him to find within himself the mystery he's been looking for, after having lost his identity. This book will warm the hearts of the young who have missed the simplicity of people grounded in principle and integrity; and perhaps will grant them permission to aspire to the nobility of the infinite."

—Jessi Colter, author, *The Lady and the Outlaw*,
recording artist/songwriter

ALSO BY KEN MANSFIELD

The Beatles, The Bible and Bodega Bay presents two portraits: The young man in London on top of the Apple building (and on top of the world!) watching The Beatles perform for the last time, and the older man on a remote Sonoma County beach on his knees, looking out to sea and into the heart of his Creator. Considered one of the top three best Beatles books of all time according to the rock editor's list on Amazon.com.

"It is his writing talent and depth of personal story that make this memoir rock."—Amazon.com (Gail Hudson)

The White Book invites readers to know the characters of The Beatles and the musicians of their time—the bands that moved an industry and a culture to a whole new rhythm. This engaging and unusual account spans some of the most fertile and intense decades in music history.

"There is something quite Lennonesque about Ken Mansfield's soul searching—his tales are astonishingly clear and vivid."—Barnes&Noble. com

Between Wyomings is a modern-day Ecclesiastes tale, where with his wife, Connie, and a van named Moses, Ken metaphorically recreates the travels that took him into the homes and careers of entertainment legends. Readers are called to reflect on the highways of their own lives, the turns and detours that press them into the heart of a Creator who has been there all along.

"Mansfield's prayerful musings are quite extraordinary."—Publishers Weekly

Stumbling on Open Ground is a story of trial and faith like those found in the books of Esther and Job. It's a private dialogue between Ken, his wife Connie, and the God who transformed them in the middle of a heartbreaking disease.

"Ken is jarringly honest about everything—life, success, fame,disillusionment, faith, cancer.... This book might make you a little uncomfortable, but that's probably why you should read it."—Bernie Leadon, founding member of The Eagles

Rock and a Heart Place is a raw, sensitive, and unforgettable journey from sex, drugs, and rock and roll to sweet salvation. Ken takes readers on a mesmerizing journey alongside members of some of music's most iconic bands, including Kansas, Ozzy Osbourne, Korn, Prince, The Turtles, and The Byrds, just to name a few. Their recollections of the way things were offers a backstage pass into a bizarre world that in the end reveals the bigger picture of God's purpose for our lives.

"This fascinating and fun-to-read book is loaded with inside stories of some of our favorite music-makers. It is a classic reminder that regardless what messes our family or friends might encounter, the Creator is greater; nobody is beyond hope, and there is no need to give up on anyone!"—Ken Abraham, *New York Times* bestselling author

PHILCO

KEN MANSFIELD

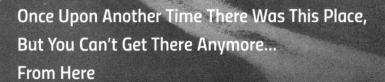

Once Upon Another Time There Was This Place,
But You Can't Get There Anymore...
From Here

Post Hill Press
New York • Nashville
posthillpress.com

Published in the United States of America

JOURNEY OF CONTENT

ONCE UPON ANOTHER TIME

THERE USED TO BE this very nice place—America—a faraway place in time. People said corny things about it like: "The land of the free," "The home of the brave," and "The land that I love." It was easy to find then; it was everywhere, "from sea to shining sea." Then, God was asked to leave and it has never been the same.

One day, while walking in our beautiful Sierra Nevada foothills, I began thinking about this change, and I became very sad. I was brought up in the traditions and faith of our country. I lived in its small towns among its hardworking people—people who took care of their own and asked little in return. Our expectations were small and demands were few. We were brought up knowing if we plowed in the cold we would eat at the harvest. We were united in purpose and enjoyed our differences.

We never thought of averaging out, living off the sweat of our neighbor's brow, or drinking from vineyards we never planted.

I miss that place, a place that actually existed in my lifetime. It was a "let me help you with that tire ma'am," "honest day's work for an honest dollar" kind of place. We now find ourselves at a bizarre point in time where each day we are told of some new and peculiar change that is taking place; changes that good and common people can't begin to relate to or comprehend.

Once again, a tree has fallen in a garden of plenty. It made a lot of noise; but, whether the people were in the forest or on a freeway, it appears no one was listening. The surviving fractured limbs that emanate from that point forward are excruciatingly hard to grasp, leaving us hanging on today for dear life.

I get lost in remembering how America looked, felt, and smelled once upon another time; and, in my meandering, I strain to hear the sweet sound of its heartbeat. I begin drifting, floating off and back into that somewhere else that became a part of me in the process of being nurtured at my mother's bosom. When I enter into these reflections I lose my earthly identity and my spirit melds into the fabric of God's nature and purpose. The people in these stories are real—I have wrapped their stories in the warm jacket of my imagination for the journey.

My memories become ethereal, time traveling to another dimension.

The wind is at my back and my heart is crying out—I want to go home.

I let go and become that other part of me…

—Ken Mansfield

1

SEPIA

[PHILCO]

SAM HENRY SLAMS on the brakes, reaches across my lap, opens the door and points in the direction of the emptiness outside my side of the truck. His instructions are brief: "Git." He sits there, still as stone, staring straight ahead, one hand folded over the other on his left knee, waiting to hear my exit instead of watching it.

I get out. He drives away without looking back, leaving me standing in the middle of nowhere in a cloud of dust. Looking around, it becomes clear I have been dropped off in a very lonesome place, but it is hard to know if I feel lonely when I have nothing to compare it to.

The man driving that old, beat up, dirt-stained pickup said people call him Sam Henry, but his proper name was

1

Henry J. Samuel III. As I stand here trying to figure out what just happened, I can still feel his presence. There was something mysteriously familiar about him; he made me feel extremely uncomfortable because he kept asking questions about my life, my beliefs, and my intentions… but, I couldn't answer any of them. In fact, I couldn't remember anything before he picked me up.

"Well what's your name? You do know that, dontcha?"

It was in that moment when I realized I didn't know who I was. There was such intensity in his voice that I knew I had to come up with something quick. I looked at the center of the dashboard. Philco was stamped on the radio dial.

"They call me Philco."

He said a person would have to be very lost to be in a place like this. But, I didn't know I was lost. I was dressed proper, looked clean, and there was a nice leather bag sitting in the weeds beside me on the roadside. I know seeing me had to be strange because it wasn't even a highway, and I wasn't hitchhiking when he came along. I was just standing there looking down a rutted dirt road, watching him drive toward me from out of the distance. You see these kinds of paths and wonder about them as they branch off and away from a long county road into a scrubby nowhere—a trail that obviously leads to a remote ranch or someplace that is no longer somewhere. I don't know why he stopped to give me a ride. I am not sure why I got in. I guess I got in because he opened the door. The most peculiar part about all of this is that when I saw that moving, faraway speck of dust, I knew he was coming for me.

Everything about his features suggested scorched earth, cold winters, eternal matters, and lonely places. Most of all, there was something about him that seemed timeless.

"Philco…hmm."

He talked non-stop from the moment I got in, tapping the steering wheel in broken rhythm to punctuate his words. His voice sounded like warm wind coming down a dry creek bed. The ride didn't last long though, and after a few bumpy miles of a one-sided conversation, he finally pulled over and told me it was time to get out.

I watch that dirty old truck disappear into the distance becoming once again that tiny speck that found me only minutes ago. I feel abandoned in an emptiness that has no edges for me to grasp in order to discern any meaning about this moment in time. Nothing about standing here as the dust settles around me makes any sense to me either.

I am certain though that his words, this place, and our brief encounter were by design. It's almost as if his questions were not based on curiosity but on some form of ethereal impartation.

I look down at the ground; my boots are shiny beneath the dust. My pockets are empty except for something bulky and very heavy in my right front. I reach in and pull out a handful of silver dollars—they sparkle in the sun like flattened diamonds. I put them back, walk over to a long sloping rock, sit down, and pull my leather satchel on my lap. I open it up and find neatly folded clothing—one pair of socks, one shirt, one undershirt, one pair of underwear, one pair of pants, a wind-breaker and a folded baseball cap. A separate section in the satchel holds toiletries.

A photograph is tucked into a side pocket. I carefully slide it out and find a worn sepia picture of a boy standing barefoot next to a gentle woman, her head tilted, her face drawn, yet pretty. The background is vast, sweeping fields of stubble and faded mountains that lie in the distance. Between the boy, the woman, and those mountains, a man stands alone leaning against a scrawny tree. I wonder if the boy is me, but I have no idea what I look like. Something about her is warm and familiar. Something about him is like where he is standing in the picture…distant. I turn it over and find a message scrawled in pencil on the other side. The handwriting is feminine yet there is a tension in the flow.

Go. You will know what to do.
You will understand when you find it.
It's still out there where it used to be.
You must go back…it's not here anymore.

I carefully put it back into its place as if it is sacred. These images, the crusty guy in the pickup, this road, and some handwritten words are all I know. I am tired from not knowing and feel misplaced but I don't have enough stuff in my head to become confused. I throw the satchel strap over my head so it crosses my chest and hold my only possessions close to the other side. I lean back against the rest of the rock and close my eyes. A soft wind touches my face.

I drift off into a dream that begins dreaming me.

2

PRAIRIE AIR

[PHILCO]

JOLTED AWAKE BY THE SILENCE I leap to my feet, clutching the satchel to my chest. I must have dozed off. I still have no idea where I am, but it is obviously the edge—a place very far away from the center of anything. I feel as though I have been zeroed out, like dust after it has been stirred and spread to new places, and I like the sensation.

This must be a prairie.

My surroundings tell me it is only lightly beautiful. There is so much of nothing to take in here; yet, I have to admit there is a subtle charm in its rough expanse. For miles in every direction I find that the sameness of the landscape gives this stretch an uncanny appearance of being unapproachable and inviting at the same time. The smell of my surroundings is reminiscent of parched potpourri with a touch of grit.

I walk toward what appears to be the tops of buildings on the horizon. In the far-off distance, way beyond these supposed structures, there are various levels of mountains stacked like jagged dominos against a clear blue sky. I am alone in this hushed place so I laugh out loud into the silence—a sound-check of sorts. There is no echo, only prairie and its dogs blinking.

"Hey!" I yell into the distance. Still nothing…and I don't recognize my own voice.

I come upon a path—a weed-lined corridor—fortunately pointing in the direction I intend to travel, I join its course and discover that I really like this emptiness. I find myself softly energized by the stillness of the wind blown feel that surrounds me. As I draw closer to my once remote destination, I can see that this is, in fact, a town I am approaching. Its appearance gains in definition, and I hear music riding on the breeze as it passes through the shanty-boarded buildings in the near distance inviting me to enter. A tumbleweed rolls out to greet me.

I walk up to the town's edge and into its outer limits. Something from the left side of my brain moves to the right of center, noting the oddity—the sensual whiplash—of a town beginning so abruptly out of the barrenness surrounding it. I stand in the middle of a street that runs the length of the town, bordered by a long row of storefronts on each side. I move off center, to my right, and step up onto the boardwalk that trims the lower edges of the buildings. My footsteps sound disproportionately loud as they reverberate down the street and seem to exit through a portal at the other end of town.

"Hello!"

Nothing…

The sun is hot and hovers directly overhead, offering no shadow to my form. I stop, stand very still, and stare into the blank reflections of darkened windows on the weather-beaten buildings before me. The place is empty except for an old man sitting on a wooden bench outside the entrance to the Palace Hotel. He looks up and I know I am supposed to sit down beside him. He begins talking without introduction or acknowledgement and I am immediately drawn deep into stories of another time when this was, as he claims, "a thriving city." A dusty, crinkled cowboy hat, drawn down over a shock of red hair, conceals the face defined by crags and whiskers. His gnarled hands, one folded over the other, rest on his left knee. His voice and vacant stare fuse into muted hues that match so closely I can't tell them apart as he paints faded watercolor pictures of the past. Something about him reminds me of Sam Henry…maybe it's the hands. Without looking away he reaches down to his side and picks up a bone-handled buck knife and a roughly carved stick—a natural segue into the art of whittling with one fluid motion—and begins whittling attentively while he talks.

"The name of the town is Hurricane Hills." He pauses at this point of information and gives me a look suggesting a response, catching me in the middle of wondering what prompted anyone to name this place anything involving "Hills." Maybe there were hills here at one time and a hurricane blew them away. I sense he is staring at me as if he can read my thoughts. I have a hunch I know what he is thinking as well, and it is something along the lines of not being amused by what I just thought about the name of his town. The pause serves to punctuate the awkward silence between these two strangers. He holds out his hand, almost as an effort to break through the stillness that hangs over us: "I'm Robbert…with two 'b's." Apparently, my name is not a necessary component of the conversation, as he doesn't ask for mine, though I do jump in when I find an opening in his pause to draw in a deep breath.

"I'm Philco." Besides, I want to get used to my voice.

He continues without acknowledgement. "Back then there was a high school, a junior high, a grade school, and a small teacher's college. There were 'different parts of town' and the downtown bustled, especially on Saturdays. It was a proud crossroads of cultures…"

He stops talking. Lifting his eyes away from mine, he looks over my shoulder and down the deserted street. I can tell by the length of this pause that his gaze doesn't stop there, but continues out across the emptiness beyond the edge of town.

"It was where farmers used to make the foothill parts of the prairies abound with wheat and alfalfa and ranchers grazed their cattle on other portions of natural grasslands. It was a place where Chinese rail-workers stayed behind when the work was done. But, most important, it was the natural home of an Indian tribe that, at one time, had it all to themselves until they were forced off the land of their ancestors. Of course, in time, they were herded back upon it once it had lost its innocence of terrain and its value to the 'white man.'"

His presence fills my entire field of vision. I am even surer that I have come upon this place for a reason and sense an ordered suspension, so I make myself as comfortable as I can on the hard, weathered bench. I listen intently, motionless so as not to interrupt his cadence. It's obvious that the telling is like breathing to him; it is how he stays alive. His words create curiously familiar images and my mind lulls into the panorama of this verbal portrait—their sound fading away down the lonely street before us. As they resonate around undefined edges, he gently unfolds a story about two boys growing up on the neighboring prairies, along rivers, and by reservation lands. His words breathe life into the moment like a warm breeze overflowing with Indian summer fragrances.

This curious old man sitting next to me has just become the host on my inaugural journey through this sacred place and I am carried away into the codger's tale about a young fellow called Jacob and an Indian lad named Joshua.

I close my eyes and am lifted off the bench and high above the dusty street from where the scene unfolds, my body hovering there for a moment and then drifting into that other time and a town like this one. The clack-clack of Robbert's buck-knife hitting the wood falls in time with his words and his breathing, the trio creating a pulsating time signature—an airy, dreamy, drum-like soundtrack—for his story. I recognize the tempo; it is the same as Sam Henry's tapping on the steering wheel.

When I open my eyes, below me is a schoolyard. I see two young lads standing around an old circular cement drinking fountain. Its rim is dotted with several round silver balls that offer up cool water to the boys and girls who bend their heads together receiving a communion of sorts. The landscape morphs from brown on brown to multiple greens, browns, and grays, and my focus narrows on the faded red brick exterior of an old schoolhouse. Joshua drinks deep, turns his back, and looks to the fields beyond. Jacob's soft blue eyes follow his every move.

Robbert's voice carries me forward…

3

MAN WORDS

[ROBBERT]

"I WAS A SCHOOLTEACHER in a small western town back then, and a real good one, most people say. I was respectfully addressed as 'Mr. Roberts' by students and staff alike, and I wore a suit and tie to work. My father had a quirky sense of humor so he had named me Robbert—yes, Robbert Roberts. The way he tells it, the reason he anointed me with the extra 'b' in my first name was to avoid confusion between my first and last—figure that one out. I accepted that explanation, but wish he hadn't picked Roberto for my middle name."

Robbert Roberto Roberts continues, his tone switching from explanatory to instructive. "When you are in charge of sixth graders you develop an acute awareness of the youthful dynamics of this very unique environment. As the school year progressed, so did several storylines, subplots, and scenarios developing between the students. It was like watching a curious puzzle being assembled in the classroom and on the playground. Sometimes I could predict the outcome, but young people are tricky, and more often, I got hoodwinked in the end." I nod from my nothingness, knowing that it doesn't matter what I do.

"Out of all these observances over the years, there is one that will always stand out in both my heart and mind—the unique relationship between Jacob and Joshua…" He pauses as if to let the names sink in before he continues. "They were both twelve–such a precarious age for young lads. It's that tumultuous time when the body is ready to embark on some very powerful changes but has yet to notify the rest of the molecules comprising the unwitting teen-to-be. Toy trucks and insects have already become less interesting, but a replacement hasn't surfaced yet to take their place, such as the girls who are getting ready to emerge into the periphery of a young fellar's once uncomplicated psyche. Everything is a surprise and the boy-now/man-to-be cannot stop wondering why."

Robbert pauses and I shift positions. "I know what you mean," I offer, even though I have no idea what he was talking about. At this point I'm not sure I know what a psyche is or how to complicate one even if I did. It didn't matter though 'cause I can tell the pause isn't for my benefit or an invitation for a verbal intrusion.

"For Jacob, growing up in deep country in the late forties, there wasn't much going on to spur curiosity or capture interest around his remote home out on the prairie. Coming into town on the school bus each weekday morning to the elementary school was a welcomed opportunity to become inquisitive about matters that weren't apparent on the farm.

"The town kids were intimidating with their seemingly perfect families, nice homes, and upscale ways. Jacob was very cautious of the guys his age from the sawmill area down by the river who postured, waiting for the least sign of weakness from anyone outside their 'zone.' But it was safe in the classroom, and he got excited about the new worlds that opened up during exchanges between the teachers and students. Jacob sat in awe as he learned about other lands and different cultures. Back in those innocent days, people in authority cared about the responsibilities outlined in their job descriptions."

I find myself leaning forward as Robbert draws me deeper into this other time and space.

"As a young lad, Jacob was also intrigued by the kids bussed in from the Indian reservation that bordered our small town. Actually, he was more than intrigued; he was enthralled. They were quiet, focused, detached, and fabulous to look at. They had long, flowing, shiny, raven hair. They had deep, dark, and bright, white eyes set against velvety, bronze-tinted skin. The young boys were very handsome, and the girls elusively pretty.

"The school busses dropped everyone off between the junior high and the wood shop building out back so they could disperse to the junior and senior high schools directly across two of the streets bordering the grade school, making it easy for Jacob to envision how they would look when they became teenagers—providing him with a personal evolution chart right before his eyes.

"The young men were sinewy, straight, and tall with a countenance that quietly stated they weren't afraid of anyone. That is why no one ever tested them. The girls were stunning in their beauty as they made their way into maturity. No one could blame a young lad for noticing that their bodies were like goddess-sculptured exotica, developing way ahead of the poor, plain, white girls. Their fine points were highly accentuated by long, silken black hair, with skin as smooth as liquid caramel and eyes that could send a young boy into Olympic-style perspiration."

Robbert pauses so long at this recollection that I wonder if he is going to stay with this image of the young girls or keep telling his story. This time I do wish I knew what he means…then he finally continues.

"Jacob's hometown was where the logs came down the river from far-away forests that covered the northern portions of the territory to the waiting sawmill just outside of town. It was also the center of commerce for all the ranchers and farmers who worked their gigantic spreads that crisscrossed the great prairies and vast wilderness of this remote territory. It was the old days in Cowboy and Indian land, and Saturday was the big day in town when all the people came together.

"The lumberjacks and ranch hands would come into town to spend their paychecks at the taverns and cheap hotels; the ranchers and farmers came for feed, tackle, and supplies; and, the Indians were there to purchase white man goods after the government checks arrived. Jacob noticed the tribal members were different than the other outcasts—the bums, cheap women, dere-licts—and admired the way they didn't look down when they walked the white man's streets. They always held their heads high looking directly at you, with those dark piercing eyes as they passed by."

Robbert's whittling has found a pattern, serving as percussion for the soundtrack of his personal moving picture, and he is hitting the wood harder and harder with his knife. With his jaw set and his eyes closed, he carries on.

"As bizarre as it may seem, this was a point in our not so distant history when a young person would grow up in an America where local taverns were not allowed to sell 'firewater' (hard liquor) to the Indians. There was a designated Indian bar down by the river, on the outskirts of town where they were allowed to buy beer. The hard stuff was strictly forbidden. The 'Indian bar' was far enough away from everyone so nobody had to watch as they got drunk and blew it out. By my way of thinking, the lack of firewater simply forced them to drink larger quantities of beer to reach a point for the pain of their lost heritage to go away.

"This was hard country," he explained, "and it was commonplace to see—just as in the movies—a wasted desperado being thrown through the swinging doors of a saloon onto the main street sidewalk. It was prudent procedure to stay along the outer edge of the sidewalk when walking by these watering holes while keeping an eye on the entrance just in case a flying cowboy came through those swinging doors. There were no bar stools in the saloons, only a long brass foot-rail with spittoons at each end of the bar. The logic and the law agreed it was okay to serve the customers a drink as long as they could remain standing up.

"So it was cowboy hats, spurs, chaps, 'chaw tabacky,' horses, drunken brawls, colorful Indians, and fine ladies and gentlemen of all sizes and shapes that filled the main street of Jacob's panhandle town in his growing up years. What made this especially interesting was that Jacob had spent the earliest of his formative years in a more 'civilized' setting in a small Quaker town back east where things were a little more staid and proper. Because Jacob's original introduction to this foreign place came in the form of 'Wild West' movies, by the time he landed there he was scared to death of Indians, and in awe of the heroic cowboys."

Robbert goes on for a while in great detail about how the young lad became "westernized," and how, in time, that all changed. As he talks he moves further back into that time, his eyes becoming almost vacant and his breathing becoming almost undetectable.

"Growing up in town there were four groups of guys. In descending order of current social worthiness, they were the town kids, the prairie kids (like Jacob), the river kids, and, finally, the Indian kids. Everyone knew his or her place and things ran smoothly. The main difference in a boy's life potential was that the two middle categories did have a chance of moving up to the first group or out into the world someday; but, the Indians were Indians, and that wasn't going to change. It didn't help matters that the young ones didn't really seem to care a lot about the future. No matter how hard the elders tried, they couldn't seem to inspire their children to make a life for themselves beyond the reservation. The tribal council sent many high school graduates from the reservation to the State University less than fifty miles away, but even with a free ride and heart-felt encouragement from the tribe, no one had the determination to graduate. Alcoholism and lethargy dominated the later years and a daunting sadness prevailed over their existence. It was tragic because the tribe was a beautiful, peaceful, gentle, and intelligent group of people. They were high-spirited beings who loved their ancient lands and were deeply dedicated to right living with nature and close family ties. They had been shuffled around from reservation to reservation, robbed of their natural system of survival and given just enough money to keep them an inch-and-a-half from poverty. It killed their passion for living.

After time, they just tucked away into the silence of a life they did not understand or want."

The aching in Robbert's heart for the Native American culture seeps into his delivery as his tone softens and his pauses lengthen. I can tell he is having a hard time keeping from crying. And, it is clear he really liked Jacob by the way he said his name as he spoke.

"Jacob was enthralled with these people. He loved the softness of their spirit and the splendor of their ways. He was drawn to one Indian lad his age named Joshua, and was especially intrigued by how he spent his time during recess. Jacob wondered why he never answered questions when called on in class and why he never talked to anyone in the schoolyard. Joshua was different from the others of the reservation who were bussed into the town school each day. He kept to himself and never spoke to anyone. He would always run away into the fields alone during breaks and return just before the bell.

"Jacob wanted to know more about Joshua. He approached him many times, but Joshua always turned away as if he didn't hear Jacob speaking to him. During the rare instances when Jacob would corner him, he looked past Jacob like he didn't exist. Jacob made a project out of the two of them. It wasn't something he thought out in great detail, and he honestly did not have an agenda other than for the two of them to become friends, even though that was not acceptable at the time. Jacob was patient, persistent, and quite willing to wait it out in order to befriend this quiet soul if that is what it was going to take. One day Jacob caught him at the drinking fountain in the schoolyard. It was that day the quiet Indian lad realized Jacob's heart was like a bulldog and he wasn't going to let go.

"His given name was Joshua and his tribal family name was Sobota; but the name that defined him was the one given to him by the elders: Ha'atya Tewe'kekeweet—the one who chases the winds. He was from a proud Indian tribe of the northern plains and had learned about God at the mission; but, even though he believed in the Holy Trinity, the teachings of his heritage and his great forefathers were deep in his being.

"Jacob was so drawn to him that almost every day he would stand close by in an attempt to become his friend. He would think of ways to get Joshua to speak to him, bringing him food from home, telling Joshua his mom made it special just for them.

"Finally, one day Joshua accepted the offering placed between them and they began to eat together, but still without speaking. This time of sharing placed them in a perfect line of vision, yet they never once let their eyes touch, though they did begin to grasp pieces of each other's souls. Because Jacob had proven himself to Joshua over time by being steady and faithful in his pursuit, and one day Joshua turned and faced him directly. His words were measured and warm.

"'An elder once told me when the day of speaking comes, God gives each of us only so many words for man, and when we use up our man words the wind leaves our body with the last one and we die…unless we catch unspoken man words left in the wind. But it is also said that God loves to talk to us so much, He has established that we could have as many words as we want when we are speaking to Him. So I talk to Him all the time outside the schoolyard and chase the wind looking for man words left behind.'

"Having told this to Jacob, Joshua extended his open hands and placed one on his heart and one on Jacob's. Then he quickly turned away and ran into the field, his raven hair flowing, where he disappeared up the ravine, chasing the wind, speaking to the sky, and waving back to his new friend Jacob.

"The long episode leading up to this exchange between the two lads opened the door between their unique heritages and melded them into a timeless pool of sweet understanding. The moment was so powerful they couldn't look at each other for weeks. It was monumental, and the closeness made them both uncomfortable. Jacob quit bringing food from home and made sure he was on the other side of the schoolhouse when Joshua came in from the canyons. They knew instinctively they had established something so deep it would take time to absorb its real meaning before they could enjoy what they had achieved in their innocence.

"Weeks passed until one day Jacob's mom made a special lunch for the two of them and handed it to Jacob as he set out for the half-mile walk to the school bus stop. She said, 'Here, I made Joshua's favorite today; don't leave it on the bus.' At lunchtime Jacob brought it to the place under a tree off to the side of the playground where they used to eat together and Joshua was there. They ate in silence, never looking away or taking their eyes from each other. Then Joshua asked Jacob about his family and told Jacob about his. After a while he stopped talking and got up to leave. Jacob stood up with him and, facing each other, they put their hands, one over the other, on their hearts. Before turning away to the fields, Joshua said, 'The winds are soft and warm—the time for speaking has come for us.'"

Jacob knew then that they would be friends forever because Joshua gave him some of his words that day and when he ran off Jacob knew deep in his heart that Joshua was chasing the winds, talking to God, and looking for man words...so they could talk some more.

4

THE PALACE HOTEL

[PHILCO]

I DRIFT BACK FROM the schoolyard and the image of Joshua and Jacob disappears. Once again I can feel the hard-bench against my back and the old man next to me is still talking. His voice drifts back into my awareness, almost as if it is being faded up out of the storied distance. Then he stops speaking to me as suddenly and naturally as he had begun, leaving me mesmerized and sweating. He stands up. "Nice meetin' ya, fellar."

He pulls his craggy hat farther down on his forehead, disappears into the hotel, or down the street, or into the morning air. I really don't know.

"Hey…yeah," I replied, but once again it is just me. It seems I have now lost my echo, though I am getting more accustomed to the sound of my voice. All I know is he is gone and the touch of his story is here beside me in this place. The wind kicks up a round patch of dust in the center of the empty street and leaves it hanging in the still air before me. Its veiled company makes me realize just how alone I am in this strange place.

Needing deliverance from the silence, I decide it is time to find a place to stay. Since there is no one to ask for recommendations on accommodations, I begin with the Palace Hotel behind me. I stand up, turn toward its timeless facade, walk through its open doorway, and head straight to the check-in desk. It appears I am the only person in the small lobby. Once my eyes adjust I am able to see in the dim light that there is a person standing motionless behind the desk. At first I think it might be an apparition; but it's a discernible female, and it's as if she is waiting just for me. As I draw near, I notice a little bell on the counter. She appears to be frozen in space so I have this strange urge to ding it right in front of her just to shake things up and bring a little life to this otherworldly scenario.

As I look into the face of this very unusual lady, I am caught off guard by features that defy age categorization or cultural identity. Her expression presents even less insight. How could someone look so young and seem so old, so mid-western, so southern, so big city, and so pilgrim-like at the same time? Her smile is automatic—appearing almost programmed with an appropriate expression, as if dictated by her job description.

"Excuse me, are any rooms available?" I ask.

I look down at the counter. She lifts her right hand away from covering her left and pushes a key and registration card toward me that was already situated beneath her palm. The card has two lines—the first line for the guest name (last name optional) and the second has a small space for her to add the room number. When she speaks, her words are measured and have only to do with the amenities offered at the facility.

"It is six bits for the room, fifteen cents for towels and soap, plus a nickel extra if you want the room at the end of the hall right next to the only bathroom on the second floor."

Although her eyes and body remain motionless, I know the words are coming from her because I can see her lips moving ever so slightly. She continues...

"The restaurant opens at 6:00 p.m. and serves hot food straight through until 9:00 p.m." Just her lips are moving and it is kind of creepy.

"Would you like a reservation?" she inquires.

It's 5:30 p.m., and I am hungry, so I ask if there is availability at 6:00 when they open. It takes her a while to peruse the evening's reservation list. After a long pause, she says mechanically, "That will be just fine," and then asks if I will be dining alone. I look around and behind me, moving with a hint of sarcasm. After a brief pause I answer courteously, "Yes, that will be the case."

"Dinner for one," she notes in precise confirmation of this decisive moment. She then hands me my basket of bathroom notions and points to the stairs over my shoulder. Her automated nod toward them suggests I should leave her area and go to my room.

I take my a la carte accessories up to my room at the end of the hall and place the jumbo-sized room key in a keyhole the size of a mailbox slot. The door opens into a nearly barren interior—supplied with only a bed, chair, lamp, and small Quaker-style armoire. It's not actually an armoire, but more of a tall, empty cupboard. I pull back the window curtain to let in some air and discover a window frame attached to a wall with a blue sky and faux puffy white clouds painted within its borders. It takes a small moment to realize that the fake window makes sense considering I have an inside room at the end of the hall. Reflecting on my vantage point from the bench in front of the hotel, I remember that all the buildings are joined together, and that the whole town appears to begin and end this way, with the structures at each end being the only ones having side-facing windows.

I knock on the bathroom door before entering and, responding to the lack of an answer, I enter. There is only one faucet so I assume the water temperature selection is cold or cold. With this simple act of splashing water on my face being my total "getting ready for dinner" routine, I head back down the hall, walk down the stairs, and enter the dining room promptly at 6:00 p.m. for dinner. I am the only customer. Good thing she was able to squeeze me in. A male version of the lady at the counter is standing by my table waiting to hand me my menu. I order the special.

I eat in silence. The food is good.

I go to my room. I go to bed. I dream.

5

PIER PRESSURE

[PHILCO]

THE MOURNFUL CRY of a distant foghorn brings me out of sleep and back into this place. The Palace Hotel bed is lumpy and creaky, but oddly comforting in the way it sags and swallows up my body. It gives the sensation of security—of being held in loving arms. Curiosity compels me to investigate the incongruous sound I hear in the distance. My feet hit the cold, hard floor and I go to the window to throw open the curtains and look outside. Forgetting my earlier discovery, I bump my head against a faux blue sky and puffy clouds. Too dazed to be confused, I downgrade the importance of discovery and retreat to the warm embrace of the wrought iron man-crib from whence I came and try to go back to sleep. I will wake up later and take another stab at reality.

I doze but can't sleep. It is more than the foghorn making me restless. The room is damp and cold, and the hotel is rocking back and forth slightly. The smell of dead fish and salt air is the last straw and I abandon my attempts at further sleep. I refuse to fall for the faux window bit, so I throw on last night's clothes, head out into the hall, and run down the stairs to the lobby. As I clear the bottom step, I glance toward the hotel's reception desk. Yes, she is still there in the same position as she was when I checked in yesterday afternoon. In fact, she not only has the same smile, she is wearing the same blouse. I might not have taken such notice of her wardrobe, but orange and white calico with a blue ruffled collar and matching cuffs is hard to forget.

As I make my way to the front of the building I notice the interior is narrower than I remembered, and it is lavishly covered with polished mahogany. Small, round windows run along the full length of the lobby, front-to-back and on both sides. I push open the oak-framed, cut-glass door anchored more like a hatch instead of resting on antique hinges, and I walk outside where a damp wind hits me straight in the face.

This must be the ocean.

I find myself standing on a boardwalk at the land's end of a long pier with a couple of docked fishing boats and a small Navy vessel anchored off to the side. Sitting down at the end of a long pier, a sailor looks out to sea. No one else is visible along the length of the pier, and the boats and the gray ship look vacant. I am drawn. I walk along the railing until I find myself standing in front of him.

"Welcome mate." His tone is warm.

He barely looks up, and then with the slightest motion he invites me to sit down beside him. I do so without hesitation. He maintains a distant stare as he talks to himself. It doesn't take long to discover he is reflecting on his days of sea duty and time as a hospital corpsman in the old Navy.

It seems I have joined him between stories, and I am just in time for the next episode. I feel like a child running late to the cinema, having just made it when the "coming attractions" trailers are over, settling down in my seat as the opening movie credits are rolling. He draws me deep into stories of the sea, medical adventures, naval hospital facilities, and the antics of fellow mates. He looks like someone familiar with the sea—turned up collar on his dark blue pea coat, a crop of wind-tousled hair cascading down to a furrowed brow and gray whiskers. Sunburned hands rest, one folded over the other, on his left knee. His voice and deep blue-green eyes seem to be searching the horizon and are unified in intent as they fit perfectly into the cadence of the lapping waves and the foghorn that called me here. The longing tone of his voice and wistful look in his eyes tell me he is revisiting a time long ago when he was a young man. I lean back against the railing as his story unfolds. Even though we are sitting together, his distant stare separates us, mirroring the time elapsed between now and his story. He reminds me a bit of Robbert— something about the hands.

The dock dissolves; the setting fills with a lot of blue and gray and I see sailors wearing white hats and clean white T-shirts under their starched white uniforms. I study their movements for a moment, then gaze out toward the horizon where ships drift, backed by a sky filled with white clouds and crying seagulls. In the distant background a large Naval hospital looms on top of a hill overlooking the scene.

It's early autumn in Bremerton, Washington. He reaches over and takes the white, regulation sailor's hat lying by his side and stares for a moment at the name stenciled inside the carefully curled brim—Graton, Paulson USN. He stares at his name for a moment, turns the hat full circle in his hands and then lays it back down. He reaches down, his motions in the same fluid rhythm of the lapping water beneath us, and picks up a small bronze telescope; and, with a distinctly familiar motion and stroke, begins polishing it with a small rag in time with the waves, the words, and the wonder of his recollection. He begins his story...

He tells me about a shipmate he once knew named Midge.

6

JUST DESSERTS

[PAUL]

"I NEVER LIKED BEING called Paulson—Paulson Patrick Graton. What I really hated growing up was when the other kids would tease me and call me by my initials: PP I did like the simplicity of Paul though. I also did not want to be in the Navy. Actually, I didn't want to be in the Navy, the Army, the Marines, the Air Force, the Coast Guard, the National Guard, Sea Scouts, Boy Scouts, Cub Scouts, or anything else that had to march, guard, encounter, fight, or protect things. I especially did not want to be around guns and loud exploding noises. I simply wanted to graduate from high school, attend the local junior college downtown, sing in the choir at the local church, and marry my high school sweetheart someday. All my aspirations had to do with a life that could take place without ever leaving the county." Paul moves his hat a few inches away on the bench, stares down at it some more, and it appears he is talking to it...

"The problem was that in those days we all had to 'go in' and go away. You either enlisted in the branch of service of your choice for four years or you waited until you were drafted for a two-year hitch. Being drafted almost guaranteed you were going to end up in the Infantry which was the main reason a lot of guys joined the Navy or Air Force right out of high school. (Something about eating rations out of a can coupled with sleeping on the ground next to your rifle was not a siren's call to most teenagers.) The ruling criterion for my eventual decision was based on percentages and years. The way I looked at it, the extra two years I'd serve by enlisting would be equal to over ten percent of my life to that point. I decided it was too big a price to pay in lost freedom, so I decided to 'bite-the-bullet' and went downtown to the draft board office in my hometown and had my name moved to the head of the list so I could get the 'service' thing out of the way. Volunteering for the local draft made me popular with the other men waiting for the dreaded military axe to fall. Each of them thought if enough of people did what I did they may never have to 'go in.'

"Well, I lucked out. The Navy had lost a large number of sailors whose enlistments ran out after they served their hitch during WWII, and for the first time in its history, the Navy turned to the draft to boost their ranks. That meant I got to nail down the shorter time commitment and would never have to sleep on the ground. I had been told that sailors always slept in a bed of some kind. (Someone forgot to mention that, in many cases, their version of a bed was a hammock.) So, anyway, there I was in the Navy. I admit I did have a bad attitude about being there; but, fortunately, I had enough smarts to know it was useless to fight the system, so I did what I was told and got by with minimal effort. One thing that was really strange, though, was this odd guy I was stationed with who acted like this place was his home. I could not quite figure him out. How could anyone feel at home in the Navy?"

This whole time he has been talking to that white hat, moving it around at certain points, almost as if to emphasize what he is saying. Then, he looks up from the hat and at me for the first time. "I'm Paul; what's your name, sir?"

Wow, that catches me off guard—finally, I am about to be included in a real conversation. I squeeze my hand really hard against the bench to make sure I am real. "They call me Philco," I reply feeling even more comfortable with hearing my voice. He nods his head letting me know he heard my name and immediately asks, "What branch of the military did you serve in?"

I answer, "None," hoping this won't become a topic for discussion because that's all I have to offer. He immediately looks back out to sea and begins talking again; but his tone has changed, and this time the story is no longer about him. I can tell he wants to talk about this odd guy in a way of remembrance—to relive something that touched his life.

"His roll call name was Ward, M.G., but everyone called him Midge based on his initials. He was slight and quiet and never really looked all that well. His build suggested he had been sickly as a child or had grown up malnourished. He wore his Navy fatigues so loose you never really could tell how frail he was beneath the folds.

"Although typically shrinking back from any sector of confrontation or personal involvement, he did make it a point to be first in line at the mess hall. His M.O. was to make a beeline to the dessert section, pick one out, step aside, gobble it down and then work his way back to the front of the line. Once his food tray was filled, he would immediately go to a far corner table and eat the rest of his meal alone. It seemed so odd to see someone eat chocolate cake and chase it down with corned beef hash."

"Wow, that's very interest...," I attempt to interject in his brief pause, thinking I would be able to react with a comment on how unusual that was, but he keeps on talking out toward the horizon as if I'm not there. Paul continues...

"The time was the late forties during the welcomed peace after WWII. Midge worked in Administration at the 13th Naval District hospital in Bremerton, Washington—an hour-long ferry ride across the Puget Sound from Seattle. The rest of the enlisted hospital corpsmen interacted with doctors, nurses, and patients on a regular basis and established many personal relationships.

The day-to-day emergencies and doctoral doings had a way of drawing them into friendships and a sense of interdependence. His workday was spent toiling alone at a cluttered gray metal desk behind giant rows of filing cabinets. Being buried under mountains of paperwork provided minimal human interaction, and that was exactly how he wanted it. Because he had attained the rank of 1st Class Petty Officer, he was afforded his own room in the barracks. There he would close himself off after dinner for the evening, except for Thursdays when he would leave at exactly 6:45 p.m. and return at precisely 9:45 p.m. He did this every Thursday, always in full dress uniform. One of the facility electrical technicians, who had to do some rewiring in the petty officer barracks building, said that he noticed there were no civilian clothes in Midge's locker."

"He was different, and I felt sorry for him because he always seemed so alone; so, one day at dinnertime, I walked over to his table and sat my food tray down next to his. He immediately took a position similar to that of a dog guarding his food bowl. He carefully finished chewing the food in his mouth before he looked at me from his hunkered position over the chrome galley tray. I introduced myself and he acknowledged my introduction without offering his name in return. Of course, we all knew each other's last names because of roll calls, duty lists, etc. However, I did not know what the M.G. actually stood for. I invited him to chapel the following Sunday in a second attempt to break the ice and out of the desire to deliver him from his apparent loneliness. His response was a blank stare."

Paul pauses for a moment as if musing on the M.G. thing and then continues his story. It feels as though he is turning a page in his recollection, but the good part is that now he is talking to me with eye contact and gesturing. This is great I think.

* * *

"We ate silently and then he courteously got up and went about his way. Being more drawn to this unusual person than having sense enough to leave him alone, I decided to ignore all proprieties and decided to make the seat next to him at meal time my new dining spot. Now there were two of us at the long lonely table in the corner. The first week I must have made about thirty conversational entreaties, and barely got a handful of guarded, single-word responses in return. Getting nowhere fast with this approach, I decided, instead of asking him questions about himself, I would simply sit there each day and talk about myself. After about a month of my non-stop chatter, he knew more about me than my mother probably did—that is, if he was listening. I was totally focused on why he always ate his dessert first. Actually, obsessed with finding out probably would be a better description.

"One day I received some tragic news from home. I was so absorbed in my pain that I went through the chow line on autopilot, barely putting anything on my tray. In order to be alone I found a table in a corner on the opposite side of the room. I sat down by myself, raised a bite of food to my mouth, put it down, and started crying. Embarrassed, I put my face in my hands and waited for the pain in my heart to go away. I didn't hear the clink of a tray being set down beside me, but I became aware of a hand on my shoulder. It was Midge.

"'Do you need someone to talk to?' he asked.

"I had been waiting for this moment for a long time, but Ward, M.G. needed to work on his timing. Startled by the intrusion, I could barely muster enough words to explain that I couldn't really talk to him at this time. Without looking up, I replied very softly, 'Sorry, man, I just need to be alone right now.' To my surprise, he sat down beside me and started talking.

He told me practically his entire history; how he grew up in an orphanage after being discovered by a security guard who found him in a shopping cart in an alley behind a Montgomery Ward Department Store. The guard nicknamed him Ward, which later became his official last name. He was taken to the nearby police station where the officer in charge had him rushed to the hospital because he was so malnourished he was on the brink of death. The doctors realized that what they thought was a tiny infant was actually a young lad between the ages of eighteen months and two years old. Once they knew he could survive outside the hospital, he was taken to the local children's home where the revolving night and day staff raised him until he could walk. All attempts at discovering his identity and finding family or someone to claim him failed. It looked like the orphanage was stuck with him, so they needed a first and middle name to go with Ward in order for him to become an official person.

Because of where he was found, they decided on Monte Gomer. Yes, that's right…Monte Gomer Ward, and the record in his file at the orphanage was the only place his new official full name existed until he joined the Navy.

"The orphanage was not a very nurturing environment and Monte Gomer Ward had a hard time competing because of his frailty. They didn't get dessert very often, and when they did the older kids would snatch the sweet treasure away from him before he could sit down and eat. He found if he wolfed it down immediately he could avoid having his dessert hijacked. The rest of the meal followed this dulcet beginning. He ran away from the home at fifteen, lied about his age, and joined the Navy. They were a little more lenient in their enlistment screenings at that time because they were in dire need of new recruits. As they had no way to question his place or date of birth without any birth records, the Navy created his first actual documentation. He not only found acceptance in the military, but also had a real identity for the first time in his life. He was an official entity. He had a name, he belonged somewhere, and there was something very special about having a title: Seaman Recruit, Ward, M.G. of the United States Navy.

"He blamed God for his unfortunate circumstances and, in callous pecking order, ranked mankind as a close second. Early on in his fractured existence he decided not to have anything to do with either of them. He kept personal interaction to a minimum, educated himself, and became possessed with the only goal he ever knew, which was to advance in rank and make the Navy his home. He was up for Chief Petty Officer and was already studying to advance to Warrant Officer. Attaining the goal of being commissioned as a Warrant Officer was the only way an informally educated enlisted man could actually achieve an official officer's rank with the prestige and privileges that went with that military class status."

The tempo of the story Paul lays out increases and pulls his focus away from the waters. He once again turns and really gets face to face with me as if to explain things of importance. "You see, Philco, the Navy was his family. He had no need for civilian clothes as he had no one to visit. Besides, he really did not like the outside world. He told me that I was the first person in his thirty some-odd years who had ever said much more than 'Hi' or 'Get out of my way' to him. He told me that today he was excited when he got up in the morning because he had made the decision that for the first time in his life he was going to thank someone. He couldn't wait for me to bring my tray to his table at breakfast and just couldn't believe it when I went to the other side of the dining hall. When he saw me crying he said it made him think of himself and how many times he had cried alone. He told me that he wished just once someone would have comforted him. Now he was going to cherish this moment forever because comforting someone else was sweeter than he ever imagined. He said if I wanted, he would be my friend, and then he asked if he could go to chapel with me next time I went."

Now Paul's gaze was dead-centered on my eyes. "Get this man…that little guy turned my pain around, and instead of feeling sad about losing someone dear to me, I felt this incredible sense of peace. I realized how blessed I was to have had that person in my life and was happy for my memories of them. He had never had any one meaningful in his life to lose before. By simply reaching out, he had his first friend and his first act of kindness all before noon on the first Monday of the month."

My understanding nods become my form of conversational response to the pauses that follow his punctuated statements. He brings the tempo back down as he continues. "We went to chapel together the following Sunday, and I could not believe the incredible look of awe on his face as the fresh message of truth was imparted to his waiting heart. As his trust level increased, I began taking him beyond the confines of the naval base. He loved the term 'exploring,' and that is what we did instead of just going places. He had never been to Seattle, and whenever we had the same liberty days we would catch the ferry over in the early morning to experience the cool gray mist and then have a full day of 'exploring.' We never sat inside the ferry where it was warm. Instead, we stood the entire time on the bow, holding onto the railing of that tremendous transport, letting the spray coat our faces until it would run down into our collars making the tops of our shirts wet. He laughed with his mouth wide open, almost awkwardly, as if he hadn't had much practice at being happy. I told him about how I loved the wind and how I had a ritual where I would watch the wind and look for God in its midst. He picked up on my rather abstract concept, and just like a child, immediately became an enthusiastic participant.

"We would wait until evening to ride the ferry back from the city because that's when we could watch the wind together in the night air with our eyes closed without anyone watching us. I loved observing Midge because he was the best wind watcher I ever met. Nine times out of ten, he out-watched me, and I had been watching the wind forever. He also had better ears for beholding the wind's words than I did. He told me all the things he heard God say and almost choked trying to get it all out because he was so excited.

"On the mornings following our 'explorations,' we'd share breakfast at our private corner table in the mess hall. He would tell me how well he slept after watching the wind on the Seattle-Bremerton ferry. His excitement was contagious. I had learned the joy of all these things so many years ago, and through him realized I had forgotten how incredible some of the simple things in life were when they were new. Not only did I relive them through his exuberance, I found myself drawn back in to their innocence and fondly remembered so many forgotten pleasures of my growing up years."

Paul finally leans back against the bench, drops his head back, and squares off his line of sight to the sky. He becomes kind of pensive…

"Don't get me wrong Philco." I shake my head left and right which has replaced my verbal "no."

"M.G. Ward was an intelligent man. What I loved about him was that he had never learned dishonesty or posturing, so there was nothing between what he felt and what he expressed. I was still his only friend, and because of this he was always very open about his feelings when he was around me. This was possibly the highest compliment he could have paid me. I was surprised at the depth and speed of our evolving friendship. More than that, I was amazed how his mind and personality grew over time. I initiated this whole thing because, quite honestly, I felt a little sorry for him. I was trying to be nice to someone who looked lonely. Now I was the one who was looking forward to being with him. As he grew bigger inside, it appeared as if he was shrinking physically before my eyes. His child-like nature made it seem appropriate, I guess, so I never really gave it much thought."

"He attended chapel with me on Sunday mornings, and we'd spend Sunday evenings in our own little two-man Bible study—talk about a parched soul drinking up the living water! We would talk about the Lord and His grace and goodness and forgiveness and blessings. Then we would retrace the years digging up the roots of Midge's bitterness against God and man, and during these special times, I planted new seeds in this childlike garden. But I never stopped teasing him about his habit of eating dessert first. I told him that life was the corned beef hash and Heaven was the real dessert, and he was doing it all out of order. Even with that, I still could not get him to eat his dessert last. He would always change the subject and tease me about how I hated being called PP by the bigger kids and how embarrassed I would get. He would put me in my place by reminding me that at least I had a real name for them to play with and that they only used words instead of fists to put me down.

"As our friendship continued to grow, I became even more aware that he was getting smaller inside his already loose dungarees. He quit going out on what I dubbed his 'Mystery Thursdays' and eventually began skipping meals. He came in to the mess hall the minute the doors opened, got his dessert, ate it standing up, and then headed straight back to his room. I didn't push for an explanation because I figured we were close enough at this point that he would tell me what was happening when the time was right."

Paul stops almost as if he is beginning to choke up and there is a slight quiver in his voice. He lowers his eyes from their focus on the sky and stares into his hat, which is crumpled now, clenched in hands that are lightly shaking.

"One day when Midge didn't show up for dinner for the third time in a row I knew something was wrong. After eating alone, I went by the barracks and found his room empty. The sailor on watch told me that the medics had taken him to the intensive care unit. I ran up the hill from the barracks to the hospital. Because I was staff, I was taken directly to his bedside where I found him hooked up to every piece of equipment in the hospital except the vacuum cleaner. He was bleeding internally from virtually every cancer-ravaged organ in his body. He joked that he never told anyone at the hospital about his pain because he was afraid they would put him on a diet and he wouldn't get dessert anymore. We laughed and then cried together. I reminded him once again that Heaven was the real dessert, and we laughed some more. It was then that he told me about his 'Mystery Thursdays.'"

Paul pulls his hat up onto his chest as if he needs something familiar to hang on to. He closes his eyes, starts moving his hand around the rim of the hat almost as if he is caressing it. The words come with noticeable difficulty now—the cadence broken and sad. It surprises both of us when I reach out and touch him on the shoulder…

"It's okay Paul; I want to hear."

"You see, Philco,…um, the reason he always left on Thursday evenings, was because in the orphanage where he grew up, one evening a week prospective adoptive parents were invited to come by the home between 7:00 p.m. and 9:00 p.m. to select a child. The pain of being passed over for so many years led to him disappear during this weekly intrusion. He knew, as he grew older that he had become less marketable, so he would leave just before the line-up. He walked around nice neighborhoods for hours pretending he was on his way home. When he told me that, I could not stop crying… so, I grabbed this wonderful little man in my arms… and I…I held him like I was his mother. Then he asked me to open the window by his bed so we could watch the wind together.

"After a while two nurses came into the room and interrupted our favorite pastime. I was asked to leave so they could tend to him. As I was leaving the room, I noticed his dinner tray waiting outside the door. I noticed that there was no dessert on the tray and ran down to the mess hall. Much to my delight, I found they had prepared chocolate cake that night. I talked the cook into giving me the biggest piece of chocolate cake that had ever been placed on any U.S. Navy dinner plate, and then I went and set it on the metal tray outside his room. I told the night corpsman at the desk that I was Midge's only family and to please call me if anything happened. I went back to my bunk and fell asleep, finishing the cry that he had interrupted a few months back.

"I was awakened about an hour later by the night watch, telling me someone from Intensive Care had called and that I should come right over. Half running and half dressing, I sped to Midge's room. When I got there, the room was empty and the bed had been stripped. I was told that after I left, he ate his evening meal, laid back in the bed and died. I walked over to the open window—the curtains were motionless—there was no wind.

Through my tears I looked down at the tray on his nightstand.

He had cleaned his plate but left the cake untouched.

Monte Gomer Ward had saved the real dessert for last.

7

FOOT WORK

LEAVING MY SAILOR FRIEND, I walk to the edge of the pier to watch the closing of the day and the beginning of a stunning sunset. I like the feeling of being alone but not lonely. Though I am adrift with the wind there is a certain comfort in knowing I have no ties and no place calling me back. I look out and away into the magnitude and magnificence that stretches out to sea as a rainbow sun implodes into the horizon. I touch my cheeks and they feel parched and crackly from dried tears and the salt air. Time disappears and only the lessening light has meaning as it unites with a wet chill. Together they dictate my next move, which is to turn around and walk slowly back up the pier to the hotel. My feet make no immediate sound when they hit the planks; instead there is a delay like when you hear a sound from far away.

I stand before the entrance of the Palace Hotel studying its ornate sign. I decide not to enter. Instead, I am drawn to explore the town and turn left, facing away from the hotel. As I walk down Main Street, I feel lost in the emptiness of this place. If there is a diminutive form of anticipation, that's what's happening at this point of my journey. I'm experiencing oddly muted expectations that further disclosure is in the air.

Even though Hurricane Hills feels like a ghost town, I find as I travel farther along the street, this deserted hamlet seems to be developing around me, revealing itself in pieces as though it is turning back into what it used to be. It morphs into something increasingly bigger as I stroll from one end of its once ratty old main street to the other. Before my very eyes, it is filling out with trees, side streets, businesses, and mailboxes on almost every corner. I find I am in a "thriving city"—the thriving city described by the old codger at the hotel. After a few blocks, I get the sense I have moved from the "nice part of town" into the "lower" side. Right about where it feels like it is changing complexion I spot a big black man sitting down on the cracked leather seat of his shoeshine stand. He is watching me very pensively and he knows I am coming his way.

He jumps down from his perch as I approach and motions for me to take his place. I crawl up into the warm seat and he begins shining my shoes. I can only see the top of his head as he works in rhythmic silence. Tightly curled salt and pepper hair thinly covers his scalp, which is shiny and smooth like polished brown leather. There is a strange "two-ness" in this moment—just him and me—and the world falls away to a motionless blur in the matter of yards surrounding the shoeshine stand. The wind feels like it is blowing straight down on us from directly above with no slant or angle or swirling. If it had visible definition it would be a softly illuminated shaft with feathered edges. There is something happening here and it is coming from above or from within. I am too off course at this point to know. I do know, even as I am sitting on high, that royalty is kneeling below.

His gentle countenance, old eyes, cocoa-velvet skin, and gray-white stubble adorn a face with history written in its lines. There is weathered tapestry in the large servant hands on my feet, the left hand following the right in rhythmic strokes, bent to the task before him. He wears a wide, dark band that covers the front and back of each hand, almost as if he is covering something up.

His motion has that same liquid movement that sailor Paul had when polishing his old brass telescope, creating an odd similarity between the two men. I had noticed his shoes when I walked up, and they spoke of a depth of meaning slightly beyond comprehension in normal terms. It was the contrast of their perfectly-shined exterior and worn-thin-with-age appearance. They spoke of loving care, forced simplicity, and godly order.

Maybe I am experiencing something more than just a pair of shoes as I become immersed in their polished reflection. It's as though I am looking into the point of his walk. I place my hands one over the other on my left knee, and as I lean forward to look down at his feet, I have a sense of privilege. There is a righteous imprecision in both the purpose and the meaning of this moment, a sacrament and revelation in the movement before me. Remembrances overtake my mind with a sort of "sixth sense." He gently grasps the back of my shoe in one hand while simultaneously picking up a clean cloth with the other, never breaking the lilt of the soulful tempo he established when I sat down. The new cloth is white and it looks like the sleeve of a robe—his pressure increases on my feet...

For the first time I begin remembering...I have been here before! Way down deep I have a story about this man. I recall being a child, and I can still hear my dad telling me about a gentle soul he knew when he was growing up. Pieces of myself are coming back to me, flooding my awareness. My dad's name was Floyd. He was a carpenter, a simple man. He shared his name with me the morning I was born. I think I can even remember him coming into the room to look at me. Maybe the most interesting thing about him was that he had these unique inflections when he talked that were a lot like the way Sam Henry talked.

The story he told was about a black man called Old Blue Pete.

He told me this story so many times that I feel it's my story too.

Floyd lived in the same house most of his life.

8

OLD BLUE PETE

[FLOYD]

OLD BLUE PETE WAS LIKE a free baby sitter. When my folks went shopping in our little downtown they would leave my brothers and me near Pete's shoeshine stand for a little while and tell us not to leave that area. Pete didn't know they were doing this because of him, but they knew he had a protective instinct for the young fellows who hung around him while he worked. Though not by plan, many of the other parents did the same thing, so it was fun for us kids. We would play in the nearby alleys, climb the trees along the street, and bother old Pete when he wasn't busy. Times were different then and we were safe in the arms of our town's common decency and had the comfort of knowing we were okay as long as we were not far from "Old Blue Pete."

He had an old bell from a tricycle handlebar mounted on the side of his shoeshine stand beneath the rail that supported the worn seats where he spent his days bent over people's feet. He would tell us kids that touching him would bring a blessing, then he would stick that massive black finger toward us and we would all shrink back and giggle. Whoever was the bravest would gingerly venture forward and reach out to touch the end of his finger. Because we were so focused on the touching point of this event, we never noticed that he had shifted himself up against the shoeshine stand so he could reach behind him with his other hand and ding that bell the exact moment our fingers touched. No matter how many times we had been down this road with him, we would jump back and shriek with laughter. He would then bend down and square off with the kid that had touched him and tell him in his warm soft voice: "Listen to me, my sweet child, and always remember what I am telling you today. Every time you reach out and touch someone, especially someone different than you, there will be hundreds of bells in Heaven ringing for joy at that very moment." Then he would dance, head tossed back, eyes closed, hands stretched to the sky, smiling as if he were in some kind of dream.

He loved putting us on, and I believe in his gentle heart he delighted in doing stereotypical "Negro" things for us—the kinds of things he knew we had seen in the movies in those days. This was the 1940s and he was the only black man in our little town. He was "Old Blue Pete" because his skin was so dark that it almost looked midnight blue. A perfect, half-golf-ball-sized mound protruded dead center from this enormous man's forehead. Maybe he was not as big as we thought; but, when we were small, the whole world looked different.

Things were not so complicated back then and we were free to enjoy and embrace the differences in each other. We were fascinated with him; and, in our innocence, would ask him what the difference was between being black and white. He said there was no difference except that he looked a lot better all dressed up in white than us white folk did when we got all dressed up in black. He delighted in teasing us by telling us that God was black, and we would howl with disbelief at the absurdity of that idea. We'd reply, "Uh uh, no way! God is white!" And his dramatic reply was, "No suh! No suh! De God is a black man!" We would go on and on about this until a customer came along. At that point,

Old Blue Pete would take some pennies he kept in a tip saucer under the seats and throw them down the sidewalk. He always got the final laugh as our whole gang would scramble after them and then go on our way, the lucky ones in possession of unearned bounty.

My hometown was 99.9 percent white European stock. Because I had never seen another black man before, I was convinced they all had that big, round, half-golf-ball-sized lump on their foreheads like Old Blue Pete's. When I was twelve, my family went on a vacation to San Francisco. It was late at night when we got there and I was half-asleep by the time we checked into a hotel. When I woke up in the morning I was excited about this new adventure and immediately ran downstairs to see what a real city looked like. Out on the sidewalk I saw some black people and not one of them had bumps on their foreheads.

We eventually told our Sunday school teacher about what Pete had said and asked her whether God was black or white. She got very quiet when we asked this, and it was obvious she was aware that her answer was very important—especially at that stage in our lives. "You are both right." She let her answer settle in for a while as she observed our confusion and then said, "You are both wrong." Now she had us going. "It isn't about color," she explained, "it's about love—and love is colorless." She stood up and continued, "God is both black and white, and He is also neither one. He is all things and every shade in between. He is around, inside and outside, before and after, above and below everything that ever has been or ever will be—all at once. Besides, the color of a person's skin is no different than the color of the paint on a car—you really can't tell how it runs until you get inside and start it up." She paused, knelt down, and looked each one of us in the eye before she said very slowly and evenly, "The main thing you need to know is that it's more than how we see God, it is how God sees us."

We never knew where Pete went at night. We had asked him a hundred times where he lived, where he went after he put away his polishes and brushes and chained the creaky sidewalk concession to iron pinions in the brick wall for the night. We were curious because it seemed very strange that no one had ever seen him anywhere except at the stand. He would always look off into the distance when he would answer. "It ain't important 'cause I am only passing through and this isn't my real home. Actually," as he pointed off into that same distance, "I have a mansion somewhere else, and if you kids pay attention to the things I tell you, then you will get to visit me there some day." We never believed that story either because we were all dirt poor and knew he wasn't any better off than we were. He still insisted that if we minded our parents, paid attention in church, and studied hard at school we would someday get to visit this wonderful place. Then he would start teasing us again.

One of his favorite pranks was when he would puff up his chest and show a full mouth of pearly white teeth as he told us he had a second job working with Santa Claus. He would warn us, "You kids had better be good because I am keeping track of whether you are being naughty or nice." The vision of a black man working with a puffy white-skinned, pink-nosed Santa brought even more howls of protest than his claim that God was black. He told us that Santa only worked during the day because it was a long drive to the North Pole, and if he came home late, Mrs. Claus would give his dinner to the elves. Old Blue Pete said the reason Santa was so fat was because he always took over right on time, just as it started getting dark, so Santa hadn't missed dinner once since Pete came aboard. He said he watched us at night to see if we were being good, and that we couldn't see him in the dark because he was black. He said he and Santa tried it the other way around once, but all the kids could tell they were being watched because it was hard for Santa to hide in the evening shadows, especially with his hair being bright white and him being so big and fat. Besides, Mrs. Claus made better dinners than breakfasts, so Santa liked the day shift better.

Sometimes I stood alone watching him from across the street while my folks were shopping at one of the stores located in that part of town. By "that part of town," I don't mean it was a slum or anything. It was a small area in our downtown where families like us went to shop—the part of town where things were not so expensive. Old Blue Pete had his shoeshine stand strategically set up on the edge of that area because the next section was where our only "upscale" hotel was located. His spot was also ideally situated close to the bus station and the downtown business offices. He would stand at attention by his little stand and repeat his signature slogan as potential patrons passed: "If you'll give me the time, I'll show you the shine…If you'll give me the time, I'll show you the shine…If you'll give me the time…." He always finished his rap with a little dance and infectious smile.

No matter how many times we begged, he never told us the rest of his name. He promised someday, if we were good, we would find out. He said it was very cool and we were going to be very surprised. He promised it would be worth the wait. He would laugh at our confusion, and then somehow, in the midst of this activity, repeated his mantra on the importance of being good. When it was time for him to get back to work, he would once again throw pennies down the sidewalk to send us sprawling in pursuit. Sometimes we'd hide behind things to spy on him. Just when we thought he didn't know we were there, he would stop in the middle of shining someone's shoes, turn around and do a little dance step while singing a few lines of "Zip-a-dee-doo-dah" that was straight out of the movie, Song of the South. The men on the stand probably thought he was daft, but he didn't care. Pete was letting us know he knew we were around.

We liked spending time with Old Blue Pete because he was funny and kind. Looking back many years later, I think we were drawn to his godly spirit and the truths he gently passed on to us. He would toy with us and tease us; but he always ended up imparting some wisdom that had to do with goodness. Take the thing he did with the pennies for instance—he said they were pennies from Heaven and that is where all good things come from. He'd tell us "As soon as you have collected ten pennies, inspect them closely because one of them belongs to God." He said it was our duty to give God one of the ten pennies before we did anything with the other nine. He told us when we gave that penny to God we were to be very careful to pick out the best and shiniest one. He said that's because God wants the best for us so we should always give the best to Him.

Pete also told us it didn't matter where he went at night because what really mattered was where we were all going when this life was over. He would talk to us about things that we didn't understand; but, because he made us feel good, we'd stick around to listen anyway. As I grew older, each new stage of maturity strangely seemed to kick off with a revelation about some nugget of wisdom Old Blue Pete had told me many years earlier. Even though these were things that didn't make sense at the time, he knew how to draw me in. He knew I would listen to the important things he had to say just so I could be present for the fun things he had to offer. He also had the wisdom to know that packaging these lessons with happiness would make them easier to recall from my childhood associations in my aging reflections. Now I understand he was just planting seeds that would bear fruit in later years. He wrapped these teachings in his uniqueness, his humility, his patient love, and his joy. Sometimes I wonder if he were even real. He was Old Blue Pete—an enigmatic, curious, old black man who shined shoes on Main Street. He was always there, always the same, and always looking straight at me when he talked. The truth is, it doesn't really matter if he was real or not. I like that he was there and the feeling I got when he would rearrange my insides.

Once we asked him why he shined shoes for a living. He answered, "I always knew that was what I wanted to do. When I was a child my favorite Bible story was about the time Jesus took a towel and washed the feet of his disciples." He told us to this day he still pretends his shoeshine rag is that towel and the shoes he shines are the feet of saints. He said the shine that he put on their soles was really the light from God on their souls and that as he worked on their feet he would pray for each customer's good walk. He purposed each time to engage as many of them as he possibly could in some form of godly conversation. He said one day he was so intent on looking for an opening to talk to this one man about God that he shined one shoe for almost an hour!

Ah, yes—"If you'll give me the time, I will show you the shine!"

One night, many years later, I had a very vivid dream. At the time, I was as old as, maybe older, than Old Blue Pete was when he dazzled me as a kid. In my dream, I died, went to Heaven, and when I got to the Pearly Gates, guess who was there? Instead of the typical glowing podium at the entrance manned by an imposing silver-haired white man standing over a large open book, there was Old Blue Pete standing at attention in front of his shoeshine stand. Above the stand where he used to have a sign that read "Pete's Shine" it now read "Saint Pete's." I finally found out why he didn't have a last name. He was all dressed up in white and sure did look good. When I looked beyond the gate, I could see streets of pure gold, beautifully bordered with bright shiny copper. Looking closer, I could see that the copper lining was actually bright, shiny pennies. Pete said those pennies were the ones I gave back to God all those years with my tithes. I looked back at his stand, and on the ledge where he kept his brushes and rags still sat that saucer of pennies. (Old Blue) St. Pete said he had kept an eye on me during many dark times. Even though I couldn't see him, he was always there watching over me from the shadows. He wanted me to know how much my pals and I had meant to him. It wasn't easy for him being different, and the fact that we kids always treated him with respect softened the loneliness. He said he and all the less fortunate people in our lives who had received our kindness were the ones who really stood at our gate to Heaven.

He told me he loved it when we got older because every one of us would stop by for a shine when we visited our old hometown. Even though I adamantly denied it, he was convinced we had all planned together that after our shines, we would dump hundreds of pennies in his saucer until it overflowed and they rolled out on to the sidewalk all around his stand.

Then, in my dream, Pete held out his hand and motioned toward the gate. As soon as I put my hand in his, the bells started ringing so loudly I thought they were going to rupture my eardrums. Letting go of my hand, this wonderful man gave me a gentle shove to the other side. With a gigantic smile he started dancing, clapping his hands, and singing:

"You gave of your time, now you get to see the Shine!"

I awoke from this way-too-real reverie and, for the first time in years, had a sincere desire to go back home. The incredible thing was that I never felt much like returning after my mom and dad died. When I left home those many years ago, it was on a grimy bus on a dreary day. I returned via the same mode of transportation. It was that strange time of year between fall and winter when it is neither season. I went down town to see if Pete was still there and was saddened to find a coffee cart where his old shoeshine stand used to be. I asked around and no one had even heard of Old Blue Pete.

As I turned to leave, I was overcome by something that was not of my mind but was grabbing me from a much deeper place. Everything around me dissolved into a soft diffused gray, like when mist rises up from a hot pavement after a light summer rain. I turned away from the coffee cart in slow motion. I had the strangest sense that Pete was watching me from across the street from the exact place I used to watch him as a child. I stopped and stared at that spot. I swear I could almost see someone standing in the shadows on the inner edge of the alley that was once my hiding place. Just in case it was him, I decided to let him know I knew he was there. I had never done anything like this before, but the minute I started dancing, I knew I had been missing out. I gave it my best shot and imitated Pete's dance when he caught us kids spying on him. I was oblivious to everything around me and became completely lost in reliving glorious memories of innocent times. I was also quite moved by the sound of my voice as I did my imitation of that old black man when he would sing "Zip-a-dee-doo-dah, Zip-a-dee-ay." In my way of seeing things, the only thing more beautiful than my singing was my version of his dancing. The coffee crowd was staring at me like I was nuts and didn't know whether to throw money or run. I finished my dance with the Old Blue Pete bow—a full forward bend, left arm across my waist and right hand behind and up in the air.

That's when I saw it—a shiny penny on the ground at my feet. I dropped to my knees as in prayer, picked it up, and started crying.

I will give it to Saint Pete when I see him.

9

DELI CUT BALANCE

[PHILCO]

I HAD BEEN LULLED INTO a trance by the undulating rhythm of someone rubbing my feet in the act of shining my shoes. I emerge rested, look around, and can see that I am once again alone. There is no shoeshine stand or old black man. I am back in Hurricane Hills, and I am sitting on a low railing outside an establishment I can only describe as a "cowboy delicatessen." The amateur drawings of food on the dirt-streaked windows facing the street make me realize I am incredibly hungry. I've had nothing to eat since my supper last night at the hotel. Actually, until this moment, it never entered my mind that I need to take in nourishment on a regular basis. In fact, I am actually not sure if it was last night or last month that I sat alone in the Palace Hotel dining room. I stand up to walk into the store and awareness moves down my legs. I become conscious of how good my feet feel, and when I look down, I am surprised to find my shoes glistening with a shine they didn't have before.

I am bouncing between feeling trapped in this place and being liberated by it. This surreal existence inspires me in such unusual ways. While I feel it is my purpose to be on the move, I am finding a deeper purpose in less-defined motion. It's like being suspended in a single place offering multiple reflections.

I enter through a creaky screened door and catch the fragrance of the food that waits in presentation behind the slanted glass fronting the deli counter. The place has the cool presence of an aromatic root cellar. For the first time since I came into town, I see more than one person before me. They are obviously the owners, no doubt husband and wife. Just as you would expect from a "Mom-and-Pop store," they are properly adorned in their white aprons, and I like the way they are holding each other's pickle-stained hands. Their names are hand-stitched across the top of the aprons. His lettering is simple, blocked in black, letting you know that his name is "Lou." Her initials are a more frilly style with pastel colors that read

"C.J." They are seated on small, matching wooden stools and leaning back against the butcher-block table behind the counter waiting to take my order. They both sport wavy, shiny black hair tightly aligned around their faces, and although their matching white chef's hats look ridiculous, they are strangely appropriate for the scene. He has his hand on her left knee—her right hand covers his.

Lou says, "Hi," and C.J. asks if I need help with the menu. They introduce themselves and apologize for not shaking hands—you know…sanitation concerns and the pickle smell. I am getting used to my name as well as the ritual of introductions and offer without hesitation, "Nice to meet you; my name is Philco." Wow, that feels so natural, and even better than that, I realize I actually like my name. C.J. tells me I am the only person to come into the deli so far that day and they were beginning to get bored. It is obvious Lou likes to talk and my hesitation in deciding what to order prompts lively chatter during the delay. It isn't long before the three of us are sitting at a big table in the cool dim light of the deli, and I listen quietly as Lou shares stories about food and customers. C.J. is dutifully quiet, bent to task, folding cloths into napkins and other chores while Lou tells one tale after the other, getting excited, becoming very loud at times, with a litany of hand gestures, eventually messing up more napkins than he has folded. It's like we are family, skipping the "getting to know you" phase, sitting as familiarly as if we had done this many times before.

After a few minutes, or maybe after an hour or so, we are interrupted by their second customer of the day: a tired old man who appears to be down on his luck. C.J. gets up and takes his order for a cup of coffee to go, waving off his offer to pay. As soon as the man leaves, Lou suddenly becomes very quiet and begins talking about an unusual fellow, somewhat like this man, who used to come into their store about every other day. I am not sure, but the person's name sounded something like Harlan, or Marlon, or maybe Garland. What I am sure of is Lou's tone when talking about him—one of fondness and respect. I can also tell that Lou and C.J. have a soft spot in their hearts for this man. I hadn't noticed where the fine silverware came from during this shift in atmosphere, but Lou is now gently polishing a beautiful serving spoon with a soft napkin using the same caring strokes that Old Blue Pete used on my shoes. The reverent, easy motion of his hands and the pacing of his words unite into the character of the story about their experience with this man. My dad, Floyd, told stories in a similar cadence—except the timing of his words were accompanied by soft strums on an old Spanish guitar. As different as these men were, there is an uncanny similarity in this moment. Lou talks while C.J. leans back looking past his silhouette created by the dim room and the bright sunshine outside the front window.

A Woody Guthrie song plays on an old radio in the back of the store. Lou is flying solo with his tale...

10

GARLAND OF FLOWERS

[LOU]

LOU LAYS THE SERVING SPOON down on the table, carefully sliding it over to C.J. He rises as if in slow motion and turns to the storefront window while gazing up and out through its upper edges into a graying sky. He isn't so much "looking out" as he is "leaving to" another place. C.J. taps me on the wrist and smiles knowingly. She leans over and whispers, "See ya," in my ear and quietly heads for the back of the room. As she leaves, her hand trails from my wrist down to the tips of my fingers as if to hold my attention. Her touch fades and she gives me a look and nod to let me know that Lou is going somewhere special. I turn to the window and listen to words that appear to be coming from a distance, bouncing off his muted reflection in the glass.

"With a given name like Louval it shouldn't be difficult to understand why I insisted people call me Lou. I have personally experienced the heartbreak of being homeless and living without family or anyone to cling to in tough times. Even when I was growing up in a stable home environment I was always worried that would happen—that things could go wrong—and so I lived in constant fear that someday I would end up out on the street alone. Well, you know, Philco, it has been said that what we fear we create, and that is exactly what happened to me. Years of homelessness in time turned into a hopelessness that created a deeper ache in my gut than hunger ever did. But a miracle happened one day that more than made up for my devastating life in the shadows. You see, what happened is an angel came along and lifted me up out of that desolate mire through their kindness and godly actions."

Lou steps back from the window and turns his gaze to me, "That someone is now my wife." He let the import of that statement set in for a moment while glancing to the back of the room where C.J. is working…and then, almost as an aside, explains, "She didn't like her given name either, so we share the bond of having renamed ourselves. She chose to use her initials C.J. to be her official forename, and, don't ever ask her what they stand for!" He turns back to the window.

"To this day I can sense the pain and bleakness of abandoned people whenever I come in contact with them. That is why my heart and my hands are always open to give them encouragement and support whenever I can. Owning a small town deli with the obvious leftovers at day's end was made to order for someone like me. This food never goes to waste and I have been privileged to feed some very fine people over the years." He pauses once again, his stare going even deeper into that space outside the deli. He lowers his eyes and places both hands, palm out, against the glass.

"I remember one person in particular as if it were yesterday."

Lou's animation and timing both come to rest as everything in the room fades softly into his story. "At the time, we owned a small but very upscale deli located in a quaint college town close to the eastern seaboard. This was in our early days before moving west. Garland was the town tramp there; and though he had never done anyone any harm, caused any damage, or became a nuisance in any way, he was unwanted. The city council and the people who lived on the hill above the garden

park where he slept at night had tried just about everything to get rid of him. He was cluttering up their pretty
little town. They were always waiting for Garland to
mess up and for someone to come forward and testify
against him. But he had done no wrong and his worst
deed was feeding the birds in the park—a kind old man
simply sharing his meager food supply with them.

"When he came into our little gourmet shop,
customers would either step aside, or, in many instances,
leave. Some would just go outside and stand there until
he left, and only then return to place their sandwich
orders. They were either afraid of him or maybe they
just had a hard time facing his poverty.

"C.J. and I were drawn to him, and we reached out
to see if he could use a little help during bad weather
spells or when we sensed he was not doing well. He
would always politely refuse, and about every other day
he would come in and offer forth enough money for one
of our deli sandwiches. I loved watching C.J. from the
other side of the store while I was stocking shelves. When
she made Garland's sandwich, she would pile more food
between two slices of bread than any human had ever
done before. She would hand him her 'Garland Special,'
and he would hold out his gloved hand filled with loose
change and crumpled bills. Garland would wait for her

to pluck the amount of his tab from this offering. Almost every time there would be a few coins left over and he dutifully deposited the excess in our little tip jar. The tip jar was a lonely vessel and received very little attention from our well-to-do customers whose demands and expectations were plenty; but, Garland always fed it with his excess just like he did the birds in the park."

Lou's affection for Garland was catching and I was all in. I wanted to know more about him. His cadence was slow and measured, which allowed for access to the dialogue without a sense of intrusion. "What did he look like?" I asked with my eyes closed waiting for Lou's words to cast an impression.

"It was his eyes. It is funny, but even though wrinkled skin and unruly eyebrows framed them, those eyes were remarkably soft and young. You had the sense they were getting ready to cry or laugh—whatever it was you couldn't avoid them or escape the tender beauty lying deep within. It was hard to get a good look at Garland though, under all the long scraggly hair, floppy hats, year-round scarves, and baggy, layered clothes. He carried a worn but well-kept leather shoulder bag that looked very expensive. It was the kind of satchel a hip land baron would have next to him on the seat of a Cornice Rolls Royce. He didn't carry it over one shoulder as would be typical of that sort of bag. Instead, the strap crossed his chest and hung on his left shoulder, and then he would cover his left hand with his gloved right hand to press the bag against his body. It seemed that bag was his only container of possessions, and his body language suggested that whatever was in there were things he held dear."

"We found it very interesting that his name was Garland and that he slept in the flowers. We would joke with him, and, over time, gave him the official title of 'Garland of Flowers.' He accepted this in the nature in which it was intended, and I believe it even gave him a sense of pride and a feeling of position. But, around town, attempts were heating up to extricate this odd man from their lovely streets. Any time a trash can was turned over or a porch light bulb was missing, Garland was blamed. All the unsolved mysteries of this fashionable little town were attributed to Garland as the chief suspect. The accumulation of trumped up charges started having a snowball effect, and this mild man was becoming guilty by the sheer number of accusations."

C.J. calls softly from the back of the deli, "Hey, Philco, get Lou to tell you about the break-in."

I look up, expecting Lou to jump right in. He looks over at me and I realize he is waiting for me to do as C.J. has requested—to ask him to talk about a break-in.

I feel very engaged now and ask with great interest, "A break-in, Lou; what's that all about?" At that moment I become acutely aware that I am in unfamiliar territory. A strange new sensation overcomes me—I feel at home here. Lou becomes more alive, even animated, as he settles in to a fascinating tale...

"One night our little store was broken into, but the thief either gave up easily or was frightened away. When we opened the front door of the deli the next morning and discovered the intrusion, we were happy to find we had minimal damage. We had to replace a bent cash drawer and a broken window. We figured we were very lucky that after six years this was our only invasion. To keep our insurance intact, we filed a proper police report and sent a copy to our insurance company. Of course, Garland was the 'person of interest' to everyone but us. With no proof and our refusal to proceed any further, the matter was closed. Besides, we were heading into the holidays and were becoming concerned about Garland, as he was not looking well. By contrast, our little village was vibrant with all the colors of autumn and the soft crispness in the seaside air made life feel like a dance of pleasures.

"We became very aware of our blessings that year after spending a wonderful Thanksgiving with friends and family…but our minds and hearts kept finding their way back to Garland and his situation. After the Thanksgiving holiday weekend, which was especially profitable for our little business, we decided to put together a bunch of goodies into a stylish picnic basket and take it to Garland. Well, once we got going we found ourselves having so much fun that we began piling all kinds of things in the basket. We put in offerings of expensive canned, jarred, pickled, and preserved gourmet goodies as well as fine linen napkins, silverware, imported can openers, and on and on and on. We were having a ball loading up this treasure chest for Garland. By the time our 'feeding-Garland-frenzy' was over it practically took the two of us to carry the basket out the door. After so many years, we knew his ways and his hidings and left our little holiday gift where only he could find it in the park. We walked home hand-in-hand like two kids. In bed that night we tried to imagine how pleased Garland was going to be with his unusual blessing.

The next morning, about five minutes after we opened the store, the local sheriff entered with the picnic basket in hand. Garland was in tow behind him, held tightly in the stern hands of the hapless deputy. It took C.J. and me about a nanosecond to see where this was all going because the smug look on the Sheriff's face told the whole story. Obviously, they had their culprit and the break-in had been solved. Now they had a reason to cleanse our perfect little town of this scourge. Before the sheriff could say a word, C.J. took the basket out of his hands. I turned to Garland and began talking to him as if the officers were not even in the building. I apologized for leaving his favorite Polish sausage out of the basket and C.J. immediately retrieved the biggest one we had from the meat counter and placed it under the lid. She made a small production out of wrapping it in even nicer linen napkins than the ones we had already given him. I just kept running off at the mouth, speaking directly to Garland. I told him I was so glad he came back to the deli because as soon as I got the store open and running I was going to come looking for him to let him know that I forgot to give him his change. Ignoring the officers even more offhandedly than I was, C.J. placed the picnic basket into Garland's free hand. At the same time, I was taking money out of the cash register. I apologized to Garland and told him that he had better start taking better care of me—he knew how forgetful I was becoming. From now on, he needed to keep an eye on me because sometimes I may forget to give him his change. I then began counting out the money I owed him. 'Twenty, ten is thirty, five is thirty-five, three ones and sixty-seven cents—thirty-eight dollars and sixty-seven cents, right?' It was then I realized that he had received the money in the gloved hand that never left the leather shoulder bag. The only other time I had seen him lift that hand was when he would give C.J money for his occasional sandwich purchase. It seemed fitting to me that the hand he gave with was also now a hand he received with.

I walked Garland out the door chatting all the time to him with my hand on his shoulder suggesting that next time he should consider that Zinfandel I had recommended to go with the salami and cheese he had selected. I walked back into the store and, after exchanging a quick look with my wife, she continued our little act almost as if on cue. She turned to the officers, apologized for making them wait, and then sweetly asked if she could help them with anything. They mumbled something and then shuffled off into the early morning light. C.J. and I never said a word about it to each other all day—it was hard to talk because we were so busy smiling."

Just as in the moment in his story I can see reliving the experience is still so special that once again it is hard to talk…he has the biggest smile on his face. After a long pause Lou's smile fades and he continues…

"They found Garland in a final sleep in the flowers a few mornings later. There was no sign of the basket or any of the food. His leather pouch was gone. Later that day we were called to the local attorney's office where we were asked to be seated for a reading of Garland's will that had been prepared and witnessed by the attorney and his assistant under Garland's instruction. It was addressed to us and very brief. The attorney read aloud the few words carefully handwritten on the back of our deli menu.

"To Lou and C.J.: You are my 'soul heirs' and the contents of my bag are entirely yours.

"The attorney then opened Garland's leather pouch and handed us the contents: a bag of birdseed, a bankbook, and a Bible. The names on the savings account were his and ours. The balance was over three million dollars and the last entry was thirty-eight dollars and sixty-seven cents. The bankbook had been used as a bookmarker and the Bible lay open before us. Matthew 25 verses 35 through 45 were clearly highlighted."

"We ran into Garland's attorney almost a year later at a high school ball game. He said he wasn't supposed to break client confidentiality, but figured Garland wouldn't mind if he told us. Originally, Garland's will left his entire estate to the town for beautification and cultural projects that it could never afford. Failed charity drives for needed projects never drew enough support or contributions from the town's wealthy locals to accomplish these goals. He had designated, in that original will, a large sum for the park and the surrounding sidewalk areas for ponds, playgrounds, and beautiful flower gardens. We were shocked when we heard the words of his last request and could only imagine how the town would feel if they knew how their judgment of this lovely man had been so wrong. What was especially intriguing to us was the date of the change of beneficiary in the will. Garland had suffered for years keeping his offering of forgiveness and fortune alive until the day after the break in at our deli. I think the town had finally pushed the wrong button when they questioned his dignity and honesty. Like the day we teamed up with Garland in making the Sheriff and his addled henchman the recipients of their own failed folly, we were once again unable speak to each other all day. But, this time our smiles were hidden beneath our tears and a sense of loneliness when we discovered what a wonderful friend we had in Garland."

Lou is now looking at the floor, wadding and unfolding the bottom edge of his deli apron. C.J. takes over.

"The old park Garland used to sleep in is now a matter of weeds and a place where dogs go after they eat. All those years he was alive, Garland had secretly funded the plantings and maintenance of the little garden that everyone took for granted, and no one had a clue. It turns out that the citizenry still refused to allocate any of their treasured funds for the upkeep of this dedicated public spot."

Lou cuts in, "C.J. and I used some of Garland's money to buy a large, odd-shaped lot sandwiched between two buildings directly across the street from the park where Garland used to sleep. We hired the finest landscape architects and craftsmen to prepare a beautiful plaza in the once-vacant lot, and when it was all finished, to a crowd consisting of three dogs and a bag lady, we unveiled a small memorial in the middle of a carpet of beautiful For-get-me-not flowers surrounded by Weeping Willows that stretched wall-to-wall across the new lot and all the way out to the curb. We named it the Garland of Flowers Memorial Park in honor of our friend."

C.J. takes the reins again: "The only request Garland made in his simple will was that he be buried among the flowers in an unmarked grave, so we had Garland buried beneath that memorial. As we stood there that day staring at the ground beneath the crudely carved piece of stone, the memory of this amazing person brought loving tears, like living waters rising up from deep within our being. Garland's memory and their essence lingered sweetly in our minds before making their way gently down our faces and back into our hearts as we realized we were standing on hallowed ground. I don't know how long we had been standing there, but as I raised my eyes I beheld brush strokes from the hands of the Master who had taken the setting sunset behind us and painted an ethereal abstract across the back wall that hovered over the park. We were so overwhelmed by the beauty we felt weightless. We simultaneously reached out to grasp each other's hand and bowed our heads once again in a final goodbye prayer to an old friend.

"As we brushed the tears away and turned to leave we couldn't believe our eyes. An enormous crowd of the unseen people of our town surrounded us. The street was filled with the homeless, the disregarded, the rejected, the abandoned…the forgotten saints who lived amongst the shadows beyond this special place. We stepped aside as, one-by-one, they filed past us, placing beautiful flowers on Garland's grave, being careful not to cover the inscription on the stone. Each person would pause before the stone, place a hand on their heart and then kneel down and touch the words that Garland had left behind with that same hand.

The inscription on the memorial read:

I was hungry, and you gave me food.
I was thirsty, and you gave me something to drink.
I was alone and away from home,
and you invited me into your house.
I was without clothes, and you gave me something to wear.
I was sick, and you cared for me.

MATTHEW 25:35-36 [NCV]

11

BAR NONE

[P H I L C O]

THE LONGER I AM HERE in Hurricane Hills the more normal things are beginning to appear. Lou and C.J. can tell I am deeply moved by Garland's story. What they are not aware of is something stirring inside that I have never felt before...the affection I am feeling toward my newfound friends. Lou reaches over and places his hand over mine. C.J. stands still in the moment as the three of us look down at the floor together almost as if in prayer. Moments pass before Lou stands up and breaks the silence returning us to when I first walked in. "So what can I getcha? Everything on the menu is fresh today and available."

I order the "Garland Special," and with the smell of pressed liver in my hair, I drift backward out of the store, returning to my place on the rail outside the deli. Woody Guthrie is still playing in the background. Even without unwrapping the sandwich I realize I have already been fed, satisfied by a partaking of delicious dimension. A scrawny, three-legged dog sits at my feet expectantly. I open up the man-sized meal and spread it on the ground before him. He looks down at it then back up at me and his stare of disbelief follows me as I stand up and head back to the hotel. I assume he will be okay with double mayo and extra olives. I look back after walking almost a block and he is still standing over the food watching me.

I clear the front entrance, and once inside the hotel, I discover my calico lady has not moved. I go to the check-in counter to see if I can get her to do something similar to what humans do. It's been a long day and I am feeling a little salty. This front desk routine has become a bit stiff in its repetition. Something has to give.

Standing almost face to unmoving face, I give into an earlier impulse and hit the ringy-dingy bell in front of me really hard expecting her to jump out of her skin. Without flinching, she looks me straight in the eye and flips me the bird. Now we are getting somewhere—it's just her and me and it's gettin' real.

The whole lobby atmosphere changes into soft ambience, with music playing softly in the background. I lean gently forward and ask, "Dear lady, do you know where I can get a cold beer?"

Without breaking facial stride, she recommends The Sundance Saloon. "It's just a hole-in-the-wall place, but it's great for cold drinks…I kid you not," she says. Though her response is expressionless, I sense an edge of sarcasm, and I am sure she knows she is being a bit whimsical. "It is the only place in town with ice," she adds coyly, which, at this point, makes her word count border on conversational. I nod in appreciation, thank her for the recommendation, give her a knowing wink, and stroll out of the hotel walking like I've had already had a few drinks. Once out the door I take a right and head straight for The Sundance, which, according to her meager instructions, is on the next block, two doors down from the corner.

I pass no one on the way, but get excited when I hear the lively music and sense the bright lights as I head in their direction. There's a slight breeze blowing down the street that bounces off the boardwalk and up into my face. It has a certain softness that makes me feel invigorated like a young dude heading into town looking for excitement. Pushing open the swinging saloon doors

seems to trigger an effect on the way I am walking—
morphing from a jaunty gait to a haughty swagger. From
her description I was expecting a dingy watering hole,
but the bar is carved right out of the old Western movies.
The Sundance conjures amalgamated reminiscences of
Missouri speakeasies, Texas roadhouses, and mid-western
saloons like the one in Deadwood, South Dakota where
Doc Holiday used to get "likkered up" and where Wild
Bill Hickok bit the dust. The bar is massive and magnificent with lots of mirrors and colorful bottles. A grand
staircase winding its way upstairs to the naughty rooms,
dancing gaslights, and happy music give the place a
puzzlingly cheerful feel.

Since I am obviously the only customer in the place,
it appears I can sit anywhere I want. I find a stool at the
end of the bar and instead of just sliding between it and
the bar I feel compelled to swing my left leg over it in a
cowboy and his faithful horse kind of way. The bartender
is standing "at ease" with one hand behind his back and the
other across his waist with a perfectly folded white towel
draped over his forearm. He is dressed for the situation: a
starched white shirt, a striped vest, and a bright red bow
tie that sets off his ruddy face and handlebar mustache.

Once it is clear that my posterior-most portion is
officially situated, he joins me at the end of the bar. He

props his left leg up on a small keg, throws the towel over his shoulder, and, leaning forward, places his right hand over the other resting on the raised left knee.

"My name's Levi, and I'll be that all day. What's your pleasure, pardner?" he asks in a whiskey-tinged drawl.

I am tired, thirsty, and a little bored. I order a cold draft beer with a shot of rye whiskey and a branch water "back." As he sets my booze down in front of me, I realize that as far as I know, I have never had a "drink" before. I wonder how I even know the words to select the libations staring up at me in liquid wonder from the shiny, dented, dark mahogany bar-top. It's curious that fragments of memories have been coming back to me all day, but in such tiny bits that I can't tie anything together. I lift up my shot glass to Levi and say, "Here's to you kid" (though I'm not sure why) and then I down its contents. He walks away shaking his head in response to my amateur toast. Although, it could have something to do with me coughing and gagging immediately after my first swig.

After he serves my third round, (and by this time I have dropped the branch-water back), he leans over the bar and begins telling me a story, as all bartenders have a tendency to do when the days are long and the customers are few. It's just him and me and he is reminiscing about a deep and personal time in his past—a home time, a growing up time. He drawls on and I drift away, following his recollection into this other place. A shot glass appears in his left hand from out of nowhere and he begins carefully polishing it with the clean white towel that had slipped down his forearm into his right hand without my noticing. The motion has a pattern, but not in tune with anything apparent—more with the rhythm of his heart I think. His movement and demeanor remind me of Lou, except his wrinkled hands are beer-stained and withered from washing glasses instead of slicing pickles and sausages.

"There was this lady who lived up the road…"

12

ONE SIZE FITS ALL

[LEVI]

"I DON'T THINK ANYONE can really talk about being country unless they actually did grow up in the country. It would be like me—a potato-bred, backwoods, blue-eyed boy—trying to paint a picture of life in a Detroit ghetto. When I refer to being country, I am not talking about wearing cowboy boots, living in a Dallas suburb, and line dancing on Saturday nights. I mean deep, lonely, poor, back road stuff—small towns and rugged, simple people who basically mind their own business and use their allotted energies to work, worship, and do the best they can to stay alive.

"We were poor. We slept on straw tics (flour sacks sewn together and filled with soft straw—if there is such a thing as soft straw). We all slept in the same room, my parents, my brother, and me. On Saturday nights we took our baths in one of those long, oval, galvanized tubs that was higher at one end than at the other. My mom boiled water in teakettles on the wood stove, and then we took our baths one after the other in the same water. She washed our pajamas that same day. I will always remember that fresh feeling when we went to bed right afterward. All of this was done on Saturday night so we would be clean for church on Sunday. We didn't have indoor plumbing until I was in high school. If you want to be liberated from an evening of peaceful slumber just take a hike at two in the morning on a winter night down a path to an outhouse about fifty feet from the back porch.

"We lived down a dirt road that ended at our barn. When I was in high school I would get a ride home from a classmate after the weekend dances at our youth center in town, and the headlights would shine dead on to that outhouse as we pulled into the driveway. My dad was not much for concerning himself with the success of my social life, but he eventually realized he was getting no peace until that outhouse was moved to a less visible location. I got my way and he dug a new hole on the other side of the barn and moved the little building there where the outhouse would now be hidden and the aesthetics much better, but no one in the family liked the extra footage added to our nocturnal missions.

"Our milk came from our own goats, the eggs from our chickens, the fruit and vegetables from our gardens and trees. We also had a confused pig that thought the reason we were feeding him so well was because we liked him. Our main meat and poultry source was derived from the misfortunes of the deer and pheasant that wandered too close to the fence lines running along our place and down into the canyons. My dad was a good shot—a frugal man who did not like to waste bullets. Mom made our soap, everyday clothes, and candles. Christmas presents were usually something that could be handmade from white pine, our region's main crop. School clothes were bought once a year, budgets ranging as high as ten dollars each for my brother and me. By shopping at the Army/Navy Surplus Store that expenditure resulted in two cotton shirts—one short-sleeve and one long-sleeve—and two different colored cotton T-shirts. This allowed me to have different combinations of outfits for the first four days of the week, leaving Friday to be a repeat of what I wore on Monday. Levi's® jeans and shoes were purchased as the need arose. My younger brother never really had to suffer the hand-me-down humiliation. Having so few clothes, I wore them out, which meant they seldom made it to the next generation. The reason I put so much effort into mixing up my limited wardrobe, and why I'd had a regular job since I was twelve, was out of a desire to be like the other kids. As I grew older I wanted more clothing options and was willing to work in order to pay for it myself. My motivation for better things guaranteed the regular admonition from my mom that 'Pride's gonna rear up one day like a snake out of the dirt and bite you on the butt.'

"It is hard to imagine someone growing up harder country than I did, but by comparison to the way my mother grew up, we were the Rockefellers. Starting from the day she was born to the day she died, the word 'simple' never stopped her for a minute. Something about my mom, who was so beautifully plain and honest, fostered a deep love, and all my affection got piled up in her. My mother's core and her exterior had only the breadth of God's love between them. Some of her other oft-repeated sayings were, 'You're breathing a scab on the end of your nose.' Translation: she felt I was off in some wrong direction with my thinking. 'You just showed your butt' was the ever-ready response when I did something foolish that other people could see. Then there was the always popular, 'Don't cut off your nose to spite your face,' when she felt I was getting ready to make a poor decision. For some reason most of her censures had to do with my nose or my butt. I decided early on that I was never going to have my dreams analyzed or dig too deeply into how that affected my life in later years. My dad never had much to say as far as growing up instructions were concerned. He was mainly there in case I needed a really big whuppin' for my really big mistakes.

"I am glad that the northwestern prairies and mountains are the 'where' and the 'way' I grew up. I learned a lot from the backwoods, including knowing I did not ever want to be that poor again. I feel my experiences in the fields, hills, canyons, rivers, streams, woods, and mountains that surrounded this remote area planted something deep into my being that is more special than anything I can ever understand. My common upbringing gave me an uncommon slant on matters later in life. It was easier for me to transition out of that desolate countryside into the big city than it would have been to do it the other way around.

"Life was simple and the rules were few but clear. A man's word and reputation were definitely his most prestigious possessions. Honesty and a fair shake in all matters was a given. This way of life was deeply ingrained in the very soul and being of the country folk. It was once explained to me that there were practical logistical mechanics beyond Christian moralities that created this way of life. In the country and in small communities, everyone depended on the support of all neighbors in the surrounding sparse society. A man caught lying, cheating, or stealing should plan to move out fairly soon after his folly because he would no longer be able to survive in the obvious isolation from the rest of the neighbors.

"Because there was a lot of space between people there was not a lot of sharing of knowledge. Most of us kids had to rely on information that had been "lap-fed" or "behind-the-barn-taught" on our own acreage. This guiding wisdom propelled us into adulthood. Some of this stuff was quite bizarre even to us.

"One of the most peculiar examples of this had to do with a family that lived up the dirt road about a half-mile from our place. The Jacobsons were our closest neighbors and a hard family to know or understand. Their two boys, Zechariah and Zephaniah, were not allowed to come all the way out to the dirt road that ran by their small farm except to go to school or church. In subtle defiance of that standing rule, they would sometimes inch their way down the rutted path that ran between the fences from the road to their house and barns. They would get as close as they could to the road before being called back, usually by their dad. When they were summoned back you never really heard any names being called—just a deep guttural yell that suggested immediacy. The old man was big, and his name augmented his imposing demeanor—Daniel Jeremiah Jacobson. Even though he was usually viewed from a distance (and most likely while my brother and I were running away looking over our shoulders), we could pretty much tell he was not smiling. He worked at the sawmill down on the river with my dad for over thirty years, and I don't believe they ever had a conversation. I do know though, that if our barn ever caught on fire we would have 100 percent of that big man's body and heart out there helping us.

"Even more reclusive was his wife—not by her choice, but by the way he decided things should be. She was a stout woman who wore her hair pulled back tightly and had a scruffy, faded to gray, black denim cowboy-like scarf perpetually tied around her neck. Although I had only managed glimpses of her over the years, either from the road or on the rare occasions that she would go into town with him and the boys, I can remember her wearing only gray, baggy homespun garments—a dark gray apron over a medium gray dress—adding a bulky gray sweater when the weather dictated. The most striking thing about her appearance was the big clodhoppers she always wore. Clodhoppers were men's heavy working boots—thick, ugly, and strong enough to kick away a Sherman tank if it came into your yard. The word on the rural routes was that he made her wear them so other men wouldn't be attracted to her. Now, she was a good woman, but I think she had been effectively removed from the social mainstream by that point. The only thing he could have done to cover up her natural beauty any further or make her more unattractive would have been to throw her in the mud and run over her with his tractor a few times.

"Because of the limited selection of playmates, and in spite of the way things were at the Jacobson place, we did find ways to 'socialize' with our nearest neighbors. My brother and I would stand at the edge of the road looking up the lane to their house. As soon as the brothers had surreptitiously worked their way as close as they could to where we were standing, they would officially come into range. That's when we kicked off our spirited dirt clod fights. These were fun fights and all direct hits received applause and hoots of praise from both sides of the encounter. You never let on when you truly got nailed or hurt, even if you took a 'rocker' right in the mouth. Over time my brother and I would leave playthings for Zech and Zeph down by the mailbox after our dads had gone off to the mill. The boys would transport these treasures to their secret places in the barn or behind the sheds. We would find them returned to us, wrapped in burlap, and hidden in the weeds along the road days later after they had played with them. My brother and I had almost no toys ourselves, yet we liked sharing what little we had with them. Compared to Zech and Zeph, we were spoiled.

"Their mom was aware of our clandestine meetings and in her nurturing way, allowed the boys to slip away into the canyon that ran beyond the fields behind our houses. We would join up for big adventures in this rural wonder world, spending the days wrestling in the dust on the edge of the wheat fields and rolling down the canyon slopes into the little stream that trickled through this hidden crease in our vast backyard. After hours of 'Cowboys and Indians' and more dirt in our orifices than a tomato farmer used for planting, we would end our day splashing buck naked in one of the livestock watering troughs placed strategically across the long pastures bordering the canyons. We didn't seem to mind the goop the cattle left behind in these little swimming pools. It also never occurred to us to consider how the livestock might feel about what little boys left behind in their drinking water. Drying off with dirty socks after our sundown immersions we would hike up the side of the canyon, and then split up far enough away so as not to be seen by their dad, and come back to the reality of our individual heritages. Their mom covered their return so they didn't have to explain where they had been to Daniel Jeremiah Jacobson. Like most rural wives in our area, she was dutiful and loyal to her husband who was her provider and protector, while having a tender spot for her young boys' survival in this harsh environment.

"Time does pass, and all of us young bucks who basically had been held back by our upbringings virtually came roaring out of the hills after puberty passed with our hormones raging so loud that the birds stayed away. Most of us had worked and saved every penny we could so that someday we could have things like the kids in town. The weekly bath ritual was replaced by the availability of daily showers at the high school (after Physical Education class), which is where our real education began. Pocket combs became as important as our jackknives used to be, and the town girls began noticing that a lot of the country guys who were shunned in the earlier grades seemed to be a little more muscular than the city boys. Milking cows and chopping wood along with hundreds of hours spent hoofing the hayfork mambo was starting to pay off. In some ways we were mad about so many years of social abuse, so we played it hard and tall, keeping our arms and butts flexed at all times.

"We didn't have gangs in those days, but pity the poor city dude that messed with any of the country boys. Now, I admit some of the guys from the country were absolute jerks. The only way they could get a hug or a hello was to go home to Momma for dinner. But if anyone messed with rural kin, it was made very clear to these people that we protected our own. One of the sweetest memories of my macho matriculation was when I was in the early stages of being stomped by the starting guard and the captain of the football team who were both "townies." After a few hits, and becoming very sure that I was "going down," I suddenly felt someone at each side. It was Zech and Zeph, and when they clenched those big farm boy hands, the odds immediately shifted to my favor.

"What was eventually funny about all this posturing was that by the time we were in our senior year in high school we had all melded into the unified Class of '55, and the emotional distance between the townies and the outlanders vanished. Government subsidies and exports to overseas markets were making the farmers and ranchers financially better off—plus the sawmill had become unionized. This meant the poor folk from the sticks were fixing up their homes and some of the kids were even getting their own cars. In my case, a well-earned 1929 Chevrolet Coupe made the half-mile hike to the long, demeaning, school bus ride a thing of the past. I paid forty-nine dollars for the car and fifty dollars for the annual insurance premium.

"Zech, Zeph, and I became very close as our high school years were ending. We intuitively knew we had to share all the info about life that had been passed down to us as well as what we had experienced in the private conclaves of our isolated homesteads before we made the big break. Looking back, I now believe every direct hit with those dirt clods had created a unique bond that tied us closer and closer as the years passed. These impressions were something you couldn't wash off before dinner.

"We were held back from growing up too fast by our own family dynamics, but this restriction actually left us with a little more energy stored up for when it came time to tackle the course before us. We were completely aware that there was something different about us as we rolled out of the woods and fields. We also knew that we did not have to explain it to other people. There were smells and sensations out of those hills we had inhaled and harbored in our growing years that could only find their way into our being because of what we had learned from living in this place. To this day, I can drive out any country road, pull over, and smell memories, soft and sweet, sad and bitter, pure and true, all a part of growing up country. We went our separate ways, but the way we got where we were going had everything to do with where we came from and that would never allow us to be separated. Time would pass, but the ties would last.

"Twenty years sped by and we quieted into our manhood each in his way. We stayed in touch and made a point of taking little detours in our travels in order to symbolically throw a few dirt clods at each other and trade timeworn toys. Then one night Zech called to tell me their mom was dying. 'Levi,' he said simply and softly, 'Zeph and I want to know if you could come home to be with us during this time.' I caught the next plane heading homeward.

"The local airport runway shared the edge of a wheat field not far from where I grew up. When the bouncing little two-propeller plane finally stopped, I climbed out onto the cracked and weathered edge of the runway. Instead of walking toward the shed-like terminal, I headed straight off into the field in the direction of familiar rooftops only a couple miles away. It had been a long time since I had watched the dust poof up around my shoes as I walked out of the fields and on to that well-known country road that had taken me home many years ago. Things became even homier when I looked up and saw Zech and Zeph waiting for me by their mailbox. When I came into view, Zeph reached down as if he was going to pick up a dirt clod and throw it at me. The gesture had all the meaning and warmth of a kind hello. Actually, what he had picked up out of the weeds and held clutched in his hand was an old baseball they had forgotten to return over a quarter of a century before. They wrapped it in burlap and, in handing it over to me, it felt like we were enacting a secret ceremony. By taking that old worn ball out of their hands into mine, the ritual was complete and a timeworn passage was sanctioned. We walked up the lane to their house, me in the middle with arms around me from both sides. I met their dad, Daniel Jeremiah up close and face to face for the first time. The greeting was awkward but country cordial. He sat silently at the bottom of the stairs so he could hear her if she called.

"The boys and I reminisced and caught up on the trials and trails we had covered since we last saw each other. Then there was a soft sound from the top of the stairs. Daniel Jeremiah rose quietly and went up to the bedroom to tend to his wife. We stayed down below for a while and, then almost upon nod and cue, we silently made our way up the stairs and stood outside the slightly opened door. Daniel Jeremiah had propped up pillows behind her head and had his big left arm cradled behind the pillows for additional support. I saw her with her hair down for the first time. She looked soft and angelic— backlit by a candle and talking very clearly and firmly to her husband of many years and many tears.

"'D.J.,' she said, 'I have been faithful to you, this land, this house, and to our boys since the day you brought me to these hills. I have always done everything you ever asked and never questioned or refused your ways. I have plowed when needed, starved if necessary, and looked ugly on purpose so you could be at ease. I brought our two fine boys up in the ways of the Lord, and every day have said a prayer for you and them so we will all be together in that sweet land that is our eternal promise. Even now, if I have anything left in me that can get up and move out of this bed I will use the very last of me to do anything you ask for you and the boys.' She stopped talking, turned her head aside for a moment, and stared at the shuttered window across the room. Turning back, she looked at her husband straight on and with one long shimmering sigh said, 'D.J., I only ask that you don't bury me in those boots. I don't want to meet Jesus lookin' that-a-way.' She turned slowly to the door, looked at her boys, holding them in her gaze like a mother's embrace, and then, turning back, she smiled at Daniel Jacob and closed her eyes. At that instant the wind blew the curtains almost straight out from the wall and then suddenly dropped straight down again, almost pressing themselves tight up against the windowsill.

"I stayed in my old room at my folk's house that night. Long into the evening I could hear Daniel Jacobs' guttural sound, moaning across the fields on the other side of the fences over a half-mile away. This time though, it was much lower and softer. Like with his boys in years past, I think he was calling her to come back up the lane—to come home.

"After the funeral, my brother and his wife drove the three of us to the nearest municipal airport, which was about a hundred miles away. It didn't seem odd at all that this trio of dirt heavin' cowboys were holding hands in the back seat of the car—never uttering a word for the two-hour drive. We just stared out the windows at the rolling hills and put away our memories like childhood toys as we left another piece of our beginnings behind. We didn't have to organize it amongst ourselves or agree upon its form. This land was our lungs and heart. We didn't have to tell it how to breathe and beat for us to understand our common bond. We knew how we grew up, we knew about the lasting things that would keep us close forever.

"Outside a barren bedroom door a few nights earlier, our souls were buried as one in the soil of our remote country homeland—buried and bonded forever in the parting words of one of the most beautiful women that had ever graced this land.

"We said goodbye at the drop off curb for departing passengers. Before they walked away Zeph turned around and handed me something wrapped in burlap.

"There were only two boots. They each took one and gave me the laces.

"It was only then that I realized I didn't know her name."

13

OLD SCHOOL

[PHILCO]

THREE ROUNDS OF COLD BEER and rye whiskey…
maybe more. Oh yeah, and one branch water back.

I wake up with a Wild West hangover and the echo
of Levi's gritty voice ringing in my ear. The mind fog
lifts and I discover that I am lying on dead grass in the
middle of an abandoned high school playing field. How
I got here from The Sundance is a mystery, especially if
I did, in fact, travel any appreciable distance from that
watering hole wearing a scuffed shoe on one foot and
part of a sticker encrusted sock on the other. I feel something in my hair and reach up to find something dead
that looks like a cross between a lizard and a frog. As
I look around I can see that the main school building

is still intact though badly neglected and boarded up. It also appears that there are other structures in the surrounding empty fields. Irregular bumps in the ground and the way some of the weeds are growing lets me know that they have been torn down, fallen away, or buried by the dust and wind over the years. I try to sit up but find that everything hurts except my belt buckle, so I lie back down on the ground and look up into the big country sky. After a while I roll over to my side and notice a washed out sign leaning against a large post. I surmise that it was probably an old entrance sign to their football field or baseball diamond.

I reckon (rye whiskey talkin'?) this must be Hurricane Hills High because the letters on the sign are designed to represent a branding iron font and feature a creative arrangement of "HHH." Beneath the letters is part of a painting that was probably the back of some animal mascot—a horse, a donkey, or maybe even a dog—the head is broken off, but who knows what animal they found dominating and worth fighting for in this lonely place? I wondered if there was a town located high up in those faraway mountains that surrounded this flat place named something as unlikely as Hurricane Hills—maybe something like Venetian Valley. I can see the scoreboard in my mind:

Hurricane Hills Horses – 12
Venetian Valley Vultures – 3

I'll bet the victory dance after the big game was a hoot.

If I ignore my head, my entire backside, and maybe a disjointed finger or two, I find this daydreaming almost relaxing. Too bad I can't just go comatose and wait out the discomfort until everything physical returns to its proper place. It is the burgeoning number of bugs that are discovering and exploring the fermented sweetness of my booze-stained chest that eventually drive me away from this untidy reverie. I am reluctantly forced to sit up and flick the mounting menagerie of tiny creatures from my body.

I rise up and look toward the schoolhouse in the near distance and spot a young lad sitting on the steps staring across the field at me. I brush off pieces of the ground and clinging bits from my wrinkled clothes—souvenirs from the final moments of my lost-nighter. Pieces of recollection from my vague past mix into this moment and I have the sense it was not a good part of me. I believe if I try to explore this further it will not be a good thing, so I leave it alone. At the same time, I know there were lessons learned and I had moved on to better things. I shrug it all off and that is when I notice my other shoe lying nearby. On the ground next to it, staring up at me is a pair of worn laces.

After a few minor adjustments, I make my way to the entrance of the school and the waiting boy. As I draw nearer and can see what he looks like, I wonder if this is where Norman Rockwell grew up. Maybe he had a gallery in town. The boy before me looks to have stepped right out of one of Rockwell's creations—knickers with high argyle socks, the old style baseball cap pulled down covering clear hazel eyes and a freckled face. A woolen vest and uncombed shock of reddish hair complete the image. He is unmoved by my appearance or the fact that I'm approaching him. My joining him on the steps is a given, being true to my wind-blown mission. He is slouched forward propping himself up with smooth hands, the right one loosely placed on top of the other on his left knee as he watches me take my place beside him.

There is innocence in the timbre of his voice, and the boyish manner in the way he moves in his expressions matches his delivery. At the same time there is an unusual maturity to his speaking, something familiar in his tone, that speaks of an older soul occupying that young body. "My name is Robbie, and what you are seeing, mister, is the way I used to look." He told me if I could see him later on in life the name would be Robbert, (with two b's), and I would be looking into a craggy face with white whiskers—you know the rest. Time is bouncing all over the place, and at this point I am not sure what dimension I am in. The only constant I can cling to is a pesky headache that will not go away. But now here's this kid sitting next to me, a child of straightforward country upbringing, filling me in on some of the cracks and crevices of the story the old man on the bench outside the hotel began upon my arrival to this curious place. As he begins talking I do a body and head check and find I don't hurt anymore. His timeless words soothe me like sweet balm. Boy, he sounds a lot like Robbert…and then I see the buck knife and whittling stick I didn't notice when I first sat down. This is the second time I have seen someone hold a knife this way, and there is also a familiar sound to the way the knife hits the stick.

He continues talking and…I do recognize the voice. I like the way my arms and legs feel as I become the story. The steps beneath us are no longer old, worn, splintered wood. Instead I find smooth red bricks with brightly painted black rails on each side that lead down to a sidewalk, a patch of grass, and a nice tree-lined street. Something inside lets me know that this is a northern clime and a time of green—a Spring, getting-out-of-school time of year. Robbie's mellow voice fills the air—it's more like melody than narration.

It was 1955 and...

14

TOBY HARLEY

[ROBBIE]

"I WAS A QUIET KID, the studious type most would say. Because of my fascination with literature, music, and the arts, I spent my younger years on the sidelines. School activities and sports seemed almost childish to me, even though I was a child at the time. I saw things differently, and it didn't bother me not being popular or in the middle of the action. I was going to be a teacher someday, maybe even a professor at a big city college. Books were my favorite companions, and on those rare occasions I went on a date, we always attended something related to legitimate theatre or movies based on epic history. There were a couple of popular guys in high school who, for some odd reason, understood me and took it upon themselves to cover me when I got picked on. Strangely enough, they were as opposite from each other as they were from me. Not only did they let me know that I was okay with them, but they also included me in their circle of friends, providing me an escape from my mundane existence. (Although, I do remember spending most of my one-on-one time helping them with their homework.) But, regardless of their motives for our relationship, I felt I was an integral part of their existence and was able to experience high school craziness without having to suffer the consequences of their sometimes ill-conceived adventures.

"One of the reasons I liked Cal and Toby was that they liked me first. Cal was my favorite. Cal was short for Caleb, not Calvin, which he would immediately point out to anyone who ventured to expand his name beyond what he offered. Consistently making an issue out of this did backfire in the long run. In spite of his insistence, and because of his splotchy hair, the bigger kids called him Calico—in deliberate defiance of his desire for a more masculine moniker. This unwelcome renaming became the flashpoint for a considerable number of after school fights. Over time he began winning more and more of these encounters, not because of his size, but mainly due to the mechanical wisdom gained through repetition. The combat honors he acquired from winning eventually earned him respect, and he finally became known as 'Cal.' He accepted that as a victory of sorts—one well-deserved and hard-earned. The main difference was the tone of respect when they said 'Cal,' having dropped the high-pitched inflection on the first syllable they used with Calico. Whether it was due to geographical, economical, or social dictates, or maybe in spite of them, he did become part of a group of guys who hung together. It seems that no matter where you grow up there will always be a gang of people who naturally migrate to each other. The point I am circling around to is Cal's pal, Toby Harley.

"Toby was also a part of this same group of friends, and for some unknown, arbitrary, and aggravating reason, Toby decided they should be both best friends and competitors. I think the primary reason he picked Cal as his adversary was because Cal was at a definite disadvantage. To put it bluntly, in local parlance, Cal was white trash. He lived in a trailer down by the underpass and, to make matters worse, he was a little small for his age in the early years.

"Toby lived in an upper middle-class neighborhood. His dad belonged to the country club, the Elks club, and all the other uptown social organizations that were evidence of having a successful business in town. Cal's father was a boiler mechanic, made a meager living, and belonged to nothing while nothing belonged to him.

"Toby always had cool clothes, spending money, and was the first to have his own car. If you were to describe him today you might say he had swag. He looked European—Mediterranean, actually—and his lean body, light olive skin, and the way he moved in his imported clothes gave him an air of confident, casual charm. You just knew he would be driving a white Jaguar some day and be spending his summers in Aspen. Cal kept himself and his sales-bin duds clean, and he worked several jobs, saving every penny he earned for necessities. His appearance and manner was solid. If you wanted to narrow it down to a single description, it would be that he had rugged charm. His appearance suggested Scandinavian heritage, his blue eyes mesmerizing, especially when his gaze caught you straight on. It was the ruddy complexion, tousled brown-blond hair, and naturally kind manner that gave him the appearance of being real and someone you could depend on…even before he had uttered a single word.

"Despite all of his perceived limitations, Cal wanted to mix in, meld in, and sneak in to the 'in crowd.' Toby always made sure Cal and everyone around them knew that Cal was less privileged than most, just in case Cal started looking good due to hard-earned accomplishments or anything else that might have made him more acceptable. Yet, Toby and Cal were bonded by the proximities of gender and age. In spite of this vague, underlying drama, they were best friends, hanging out together in a tight-knit gang of sorts. Cal didn't want to have a competition; he just wanted to gain some kind of momentum out of his common existence and be a part of the guys at school—not the purest of motives on his part, but being pals with Toby Harley did help. It was always there though—this jousting match between them—and, in time I became Robbie, the referee, in their lives. The dynamics of our three-way relationship were crazy, especially the fact that, deep down, it was our differences that became the glue that held us together. I had accepted long ago that no one would be looking at me when the three of us walked down the street. They walked in stride and were striking in their difference—Toby's head tossed back with the beginning of a grin on his face and Cal, always looking straight ahead and sure, with his jaw and his expression fixed in a welcoming manner.

"Cal worked hard loading trucks at the local Coca-Cola distribution center part-time after school and full-time in the summers, and he grew to be stronger than Toby. As they got older, the only way he maintained some sense of status with Toby was by beating him in foot races, arm wrestling, and making the football team when Toby did not. But, while Cal was working until 3:00 a.m. at the local Chinese restaurant on weekends, Toby was getting a restful night's sleep so he could wake refreshed to go golfing with his father on Sunday mornings at the country club.

"After working and saving his money over the years, Cal was finally able to buy an old, but well-kept pickup truck, while Toby's dad bought him his second car—a shiny new pewter green Desoto convertible with whitewall balloon tires. The routine after ball games and weekend dances was to take their freshly waxed cars and trophy dates to the local hang out, Lou's Drive-In. Toby would pull up with the top down, no matter what time of year it was, and smugly order a deluxe cheeseburger with double curly fries, a milk shake, and dusty donut holes for himself and his date. Cal usually ordered a small coke and a bag of chips, saying he wasn't hungry while hoping his date didn't have a big appetite. Because he was paying his own way for necessities in life, these were smaller luxuries he knew he had to forgo at the time.

"Toby made fun of Cal's clothes in front of girls and often found a way to bring up his grease-stained father to make sure there was no comparison in their social standing. For good measure, he casually slipped in the difference in the location of their residences and his dad's status as a successful downtown businessman just in case Cal was getting a little more attention from a girl than he was. Of course, these subtle slights stung, but Cal didn't expend energy on the backhand annoyances, and it actually inspired him to work harder. His mom and dad made it very clear that nobody was ever going to give him anything. If he wanted something, then the natural attachment to that desire was giving up frivolous pleasures, and putting in long hours of hard, menial work.

"When Cal made his way out of town at the age of seventeen, not only was he escaping his station in life, but he was also distancing himself from Toby Harley and the niche he had inherited. He needed to shake the poor working-class badge of distinction Toby and some of the other townies had forced him to wear, though their competition did have a sudden death tournament ending on the day Cal left town on a bus heading south. With Cal gone, the game was called off due to lack of participants. He and I kept in touch, but it was ten years before I would see him again. I had been only an observer up to that point. To hear Cal tell it, the story goes something like this...

[CAL]

"I EXPERIENCED A LOT OF the usual growing up pain when I was young, but the odd thing about all of this is that as I look back at it over a half-century later, it seems I only remember the wonderful things of our energetic youth. I am not sure what actually drew Toby and me to each other and I admit he was a tough row to hoe as a friend at times; but, now my main memories are of midnight drag races with him and our other pals in the open wheat fields outside of town after they had been plowed and harrowed. The drag races and other contests were where our underlying competition really paid off. Even though he had the apparent advantages in our relationship, I was not the only one with insecurities, so we teamed up and our unified role became that of the daredevil duo. We were mutually crazy, needing attention. I wonder now if that's what brought us together. Toby and I not only enjoyed the thrill of it all, but we liked the notoriety we shared in being the rogue champions of this category. Neither of us was very big, but together we stood tall among men when the risky challenges were thrown out into the middle of a boring day. The rest of the gang knew where to delve when a little excitement was needed.

"Toby and I often got into fistfights behind the Youth Activity Center, which, ironically, was built to keep us out of trouble. We sneaked our first smokes together in the bushes that bordered the park—where we were supposed to be doing research at the local library—and were busted by the librarian. We skipped school and got caught every time. We learned that crime doesn't pay our first time out when we were arrested trying to siphon gas from delivery trucks behind the bakery. It had gotten to the point that if one of us got in trouble the other was automatically called into the principal's office. Throwing water balloons at passing cars from the roof of the Five & Dime store on Main Street was considered a major crime wave. Nailing an open convertible operated by a local bigwig moved this act from a misdemeanor to a felony in the eyes of the small town Gestapo. But, this was as bad as it got in those days.

"My favorite memories are of warm summer evenings spent standing around a beach fire along a clear water river with Toby and the guys sharing our first ill-gotten beers. The roaring river flowing alongside our runnings at life bring a sweet smell and sound to my remembrances. Although the competition seemed underlying and central to our relationship, the majority of the time was spent in feeling our muscles grow and sharing new territory in our explorations of girls, neighboring towns, and rebel music. Looking back, I realize now that without Toby and a few other sidekicks that fill my memories, it would have been rather drab growing up in the middle of Nowheresville, USA.

"I was intrigued by California and escaped to that magical place through magazines and music before I was out of grade school. I knew things would be different for me there, so as soon as I graduated from high school, I headed south to live in the sparkling Golden State. It turned out to be a good fit for me. I did well, bought a nice house in the Hollywood Hills, and didn't come back until our ten-year high school reunion. Everyone was there except Toby Harley. I asked around at the dinner dance and was told he still lived in town but had dropped out of the social scene after his dad died. I asked for his phone number but struck out until I found someone who was able to give me his work address. I was flying high in the entertainment business and basking in the glory of being a big star in my hometown in the middle of cowboy land at the time of the reunion. As close as we had been growing up, I was still harboring some old hurts against Toby over how he used to make me feel inferior in front of people. I sure didn't want to waste this serendipitous moment without including an updated side-by-side comparison of our current accomplishments.

"Around noon the next day, I pulled up in my new Mercedes to the curb in front of the used car lot where Toby worked, with my new Hollywood starlet wife poised dramatically at my side. There he was—a polyester-clad salesman at a low-end, dingy, used-car lot in a small town. It was still Toby and Cal that day, but we both knew that high school was out. I didn't stay too long—just long enough to see the anguish in his eyes.

"I had waited for that moment of sweet revenge for over a decade. All I remember now is the two of us looking at the ground as we talked, both of us aware of his dusty scuffed boots and my polished imports. As I drove away from that used car lot, I wondered why I didn't feel good inside.

"I had dreamed about that moment for years, and when it finally happened there was absolutely no joy. I know now over the passage of years that revenge was not the key to my happiness. Because of the inherent goodness God has placed in each of us, I was thrown off-balance that day. We had been raised in the same stretch of real estate in a quiet corner of America, but Toby had been brought up with abundance and a lack of guidance that, in the long run, left him ill-prepared for the real world.

When his family fortune fell apart, he could not maintain the lifestyle to which he was accustomed. By working for his dad when he felt like it, in a small town environment, he was left with few competitive skills when it came to making his way in the dog-eat-dog outside world. His main talent was participating in the excessive consumption of the family wealth. What I had seen as my lack was actually a gift, a common man's work ethic that helped me understand that if I was going to participate in the harvest I had to plow in the cold. I had learned early in life that there would be no unearned gift baskets.

"As I reflect on our youthful rivalry, I realized that the time spent in heated encounters drew us deeper into each other's souls. It was almost as if in our wrestling with each other we had mixed our sweat and blood in an unintended blood-brother ritual. I believe now that we unconsciously chose each other to struggle in the confused midst of our beginnings because deep down we trusted each other in some ethereal way. I had let his put downs and our grappling for identity fill my life with unresolved resentment for many years, but he was just spreading his wings as I was and making room for himself in the environment we had inherited. I am not sure now who the bad guy was in this situation—or if there was one.

"I realize I truly hurt him that day with my appearance and appearances. I am eternally sorry for that. I had returned to a special place of innocence and honesty, virtually strutting into what I now deemed a little backwater town. I came rolling in like a conquering hero displaying all of my shallow worldly treasures gathered from a darker place that I now called home. I had dragged my bad stuff into pristine remembrances—tainted tin trophies, tarnished by a new set of standards I had adopted from my life in a cutthroat world.

"The day I stood there in my old hometown in that used car lot, I thought I was on top of the world, not realizing I was actually at the bottom of what I was all about. I had blasphemed the significance of where I was blessed to spend my youth. I had taken everything about this beautiful place and boiled it down to the sad point of getting even. If this is what I had gotten out of all those years since I left my native soil, then I had destroyed its magnificence in my self-proclaimed advancement to royalty. I had been traveling to that moment since the day I left home. I should have stayed away.

"I was once told that every man God brings into my life is for a good purpose, and, in eternal matters, that no man is my enemy. Eventually each one is my friend. Today I thank Toby for the madness, the memories, and the moments we shared. He is a part of my history, and he did well.

"God bless you Toby Harley, wherever you are. I miss us."

15

WOOD WINDS

[PHILCO]

I AM AWAKENED BY what sounds like a window banging at the mercy of the wind. I get up to check it out when I suddenly smell the fresh scent of pine filling the stark corners of my hotel room. I move over to the fluttering curtains, and instead of a hard wall with sky blue paint and faux puffy clouds, I find myself looking out into a three-dimensional canvas filled with a thousand shades of green and muted dark brown accents. As I stare into the woods outside this once solid portal, I feel the wind pulling away instead of blowing in. It is asking me to drift into its soaring promise of something fresh, and to experience finely woven adventure among the pines. I dress in a hurry, the smell of greenery and pine needles clinging to my nostrils, making sure I don't lose sight of what lies ahead.

I am excited and I take the stairs down to the lobby two at a time. Once there, I wonder if I made a wrong turn at the end of my hall because I find myself in a large room with a massive stone fireplace, crackling fire, colorful blankets, and rugs strewn throughout. I look around the large, lodge-like room—no desk or clerk or dining room in sight—and head for the front door. I walk outside into the smells and wooded portrait I saw from my window, but when I turn around to look back at the lodge it is no longer there. I turn back to the trees and stare in wonder...

This must be a forest.

As I approach its interior, a certain calm engulfs me with a scented warmth and blanketed security. I am dwarfed by the tall trees that stand by my side—textured sentries guarding my arrival into their realm. Once again the wind has brought me somewhere unfamiliar, and I like being in this space. I have the underlying sense that it would be just fine to never move away from the padded pine needle floor beneath me. Everything has come to a standstill. I remain silent still taking it all in, and my head begins to turn slowly from side to side as I try to pull together everything in my field of vision with deep clarity and consideration. I am new at this; but, because I am traveling with the wind, I know I am safe. I breathe in and fill my nostrils with the excitement and great anticipation for what lies within the depths of these woods.

My eyes slowly adjust, and it is almost as if my vision becomes educated by repeated scanning of the minutiae in this verdant enclosure. Details begin to emerge—the blur clears and the perimeter develops sharper edges. The woodland intricacy that encompasses me emerges through the more precisely defined elements. I notice a slender opening between the trunks and low limbs where I can make out what appears to be a clearing only yards away. I move for the first time, walking almost silently, except for a soft crunch as the years of needles and molded leaves beneath my feet cushion my way. It is a small clearing and a green field opens up ahead.

This must be a meadow.

Emerging out of the forest to its lush green edge, I am drawn from my reverie into the realization that I am not the only human being here. Sitting on a fallen log on the other edge of the meadow is a man, obviously a woodsman by the way he is dressed—buttoned-up, green-and-red-checkered Pendleton shirt, and hunters cap with a large bill and side flaps that hang loose to the side, framing a chiseled face covered in whiskers. You can feel the hours of hard work in his calloused hands—one folded over the other on his left knee. He looks up and beckons with a nod of his head for me to sit down beside him. "Hello, stranger, my name is Forrest." He begins talking as if we were common folk, settling down together to share a few easy moments in the embrace of the dense foliage that surrounds us. He allows only the slightest pause between his introduction and discourse, drawing me immediately into stories of the forest, the beauty of its heart, and the contrast of the world outside. His voice and vacant stare pierce deep into the woods...

Sometime during this brief interlude, he has picked up a small hatchet from the ground and is sharpening its cutting edge with his spit on a smooth whetstone. The motion is circular and sure— a continuous tempo, not unlike Levi polishing the shot glass. These two men, so incredibly different, yet somehow tied together. Their voices unique, yet both speak from their hearts creating a soft echo in their banter.

He leans back, speaking as if to the sky and recalls something very special that took place here. It had to do with an unusual combination of separation and family unity. Basking in the sweetness of the setting, I soak up his narrative following the flow of his words and melding into the scene. Forrest's narrative unfolds as he begins describing a being that comes as close as to what God intended for all of us to be as anything I have ever experienced.

"By the way, you can call me Philco," I tell him…

16

RAINBOW DROPS IN THE AIR

[FORREST]

"I AM A MAN OF the woodlands and I am glad my name is Forrest—it seems to fit the setting. In choosing a silent and single life, I have adopted a degree of discretion regarding my observations. There is a quiet and reserved magnificence that can only be found in the depths of the glades and wooded glens. This is where I reside…loneliness is my only, and because of the way I am, best friend. I can tell you this story, but I can't explain why I know certain particulars about these people. I am a simple man, so I understand that the beauty of what I have witnessed lies not only in its setting, but in its simplicity.

"I can see her now…

"She's lovely—an expert on the depths and beauty of the forest and its ways. Sureign is her name—a name with no known origin, a name that sounds like the things around and inside her. It is a name that only she and her fathers know and connects them in a way that only they understand. It is not a given name but one that came out of the solitude and beauty of the forest.

"Sureign and her father lived deep in the forest. He was a powerful, godly giant of a man, and she was his young, beautiful daughter. They lived among the tall trees and rich foliage that surrounded and protected them from the world outside. When she was still a small baby her mother had passed on at the hands of something cruel in the world outside, and her father was so embittered at the way things had turned out that he vowed nothing would ever harm her or that evil would ever touch the face of his only child.

"He would leave each morning to earn provision, knowing she was safe in the deep and dense woodland sheltered from harm by her natural awareness and that God would watch over her as she played in the groves. He was assured she would always be safe—her location kept her hidden from any outside intrusions that could attempt to bring harm into her life.

"Sureign was extremely happy because she only knew about life in the forest and she spent her days alone, dancing among the trees, going down to the small creeks where she would splash sweet spring water in her face, laughing out loud as she threw its rainbow drops into the air. She ran with white wolves down secret trails into cool ravines, and when exhausted she would lie down, face-up in the grasses of the forest floor and wait for the sun to arrive directly overhead so she could feel it shine straight down through the trees.

"No one ever met Sureign while she was growing up—she remained hidden from the outside world, beautiful, unique, and comfortable in this protected space created by her father. She talked to no one except her earthly father and her Heavenly Father's Spirit inside.

"At night they would build three big fires outside their hand-hewn cabin and call them the Trinity. He would tell her great things of wisdom and truth and then they would fall asleep on the leaves between the fires. When the flames died out, the cold announced the morning. He told her on these timeless evenings in the light of the long-burning fires about the day he would no longer be there for her. He told her she would finally get to feel God on that day and that God would touch her face to let her know He was with her.

"He also told Sureign she would know exactly what to do because God would come to care for her and He would guide her to her next destination where she would have abundant provision and, knowing about her favorite pastime, he assured her that she would always have rainbow drops in the air. Sureign knew these things would be just as he said because she had learned she could trust everything her father had taught her. Her greatest possessions were his words and his promises and her Heavenly Father's Word and His promises.

"Sureign would often think of her Heavenly Father and His Son and His Spirit that dwelled deep in her heart during silent times spent alone in the familiar warmth of her surroundings. A soothing peace comforted her from within even though she had no one to share her thoughts with. During these special times she would lie back quietly between the trees on prepared piles of fallen leaves while looking up into a clear blue sky, trying to imagine how God's touch was going to feel.

"In Sureign's world there was no beginning, no history, no pending eventuality. It was simply about the trees and the living sounds that filled her senses. She had always been in the forest and the forest had been a part of her for all existing time in her awareness. The forest she knew had its own sounds and smells with no interference from the outside world—not once was the stillness broken by anything other than its own tendering.

"Though her English was perfect, she needed very few words, as there was so little to know or discuss. She knew about the Son and His ways and had been taught about the people in His life and stories about all that He had gone through. She also knew her fathers—both earthly and Heavenly—and she loved sitting at the feet of her forest father as he delighted her with fascinating stories about her forever Father. They were her world and she was pleased and satisfied with these few things.

"She had the wind, and it was her daily companion. It would sing to her as it made its way through the branches that touched the sky above her. It would dance before her in the leaves and shadows of the forest floor and stop to embrace her in the rare moments when she experienced a curious sense of the aloneness of her existence. It would cool her when she was warm, and it would play with her, spreading the mist as she made her rainbow drops in the air.

"Her earthly father was a man of stature and presence. He also needed no name other than the soft sound she spoke when she called him father. This too, like Sureign, was more of a resonance and uttered essence that portrayed the deep love they shared. It was more projection than speaking.

"The deep wounds he had experienced molded him into austere quietude and focus. She was his remaining treasure and his single purpose was her well-being and protection. Sureign did know that something tragic had taken her mother from them, but chose not to wonder or inquire about what had happened. It was a time and place she didn't understand. Sometimes she wished she had a face to remember, but the simplicity of her existence didn't prompt thoughts of sadness, worry, or lack. She had learned that her fathers would reveal things to her at the proper times; and, until those times, unknown matters were of no concern to her.

"She never knew where her earthly father went each day. When he returned in the late afternoon, he would bring food stuffed in the leather satchel that seemed to be his only worldly possession other than the clothes he wore. He would remove all wrappers and packaging before coming back into the woods and carefully place each item in swaths of soft white linen that she would wash in the stream after they ate and hang them out to dry. This was their daily meal. During the day, if she had need, she would drink from different springs, pluck watercress from their edges, and cherish the special times when she would stumble upon honey bees and their sweet creation. The seeming endless supply of berries, nuts, and juicy, deep earth roots were a veritable candy store. The seclusion of her existence kept her desires limited to her experiences.

"While she was not raised by wolves, she was raised within their realm, and they grew together in awareness. They came in and out of each other's lives, at times only by curiosity, and at others because they shared the same environment. But, mostly it was because they were a blended part of this sanctuary and there was a trustworthiness they could sense in each other. They shared what people try to own.

"There was a gentle ravine in the forest with a little waterfall at its head, and the hillside that ran to its base was one of her favorite places to play. She would roll down the grassy slope to the edge of the small pool beneath the waterfall, her laughter filling the spaces between the trees while the animals watched from the secrecy of the glades. When exhausted from her play, she would stand under the waterfall washing the leaves and pine needles from her hair and throw handfuls of the clear water that ran off her shoulders out into the sunlight and watch it sparkle in the air. When the sun was shining down through the trees at just the right angle, she could actually create rainbows. Then she would lie on the rocks beside the stream to dry off and close her eyes to rest in the promises that these rainbows brought to mind.

"She could hear her father coming from far away in the woods in the afternoons—sometimes she could 'hear' him before she could actually hear him. He would always whisper her name as he made his way to their place in a shadowed glen. She loved this time of transitioning from being alone to being in the secure warmth he offered when they were together. They would take walks before their meal, usually with her as the guide, revealing her discoveries of the day. When they came to a resting place, she would sit at his feet as he told her stories of her Heavenly Father and His creation and the lessons to be had from their telling. Without knowing, she was being prepared.

"After their evening meal, and as the darkness fell, he would build the fires around them and they would talk, and then they would pray. These words would lead them into their rest. In the morning, she would awake to a kiss on the top of her head, but would keep her eyes closed as he prayed the day into its beginning and then listen to his leaving through the trees. When she arose, she would immediately go to the small table outside their shelter knowing that he always left a treat withheld from the night before and a message from her Heavenly Father to guide her into her day.

"Then one day her father did not return, and that night she built the fires by herself. Sureign woke up alone in the morning chill, and after washing her face in the stream in the glade she walked out of the forest and came upon her first meadow. She was amazed at its open beauty, but it was in this beautiful setting that she experienced loss, fear, and pain; and, for the first time in her life she cried, tears of innocence streaming down her face.

"Sureign looked out across the meadow at the wondrous hills beyond and she asked God to let her feel Him now, just as her father said He would at this foretold time in her life. Then a sudden wind came across the green, caressing her face and drying her tears. And when the wind wrapped itself around her shoulders she knew that for all time her fathers had kept their promises and that she would be okay.

"Weeping inward, facing skyward she laid down in the middle of the meadow to wait. That's when she felt the soft wind on her face she had been told about. Sureign closed her eyes and whispered from her heart:

"My God, You have the softest hands."

17

CENTER STAGE

[PHILCO]

JUST BEFORE DAWN, I AM awakened by a dry silence. The serenity and tapestry of the forest is now replaced by the stillness and bland air of a seventy-five-cent room at the end of a dowdy hallway. Even though I am surrounded by an obtuse nothingness in my room at the Palace Hotel, I am beginning to enjoy an anticipation that engulfs me as I wake up each morning. I think what appeals to me about the starkness of the room's interior is that it presents a blank canvas for my imagination to draw upon as I merge into each new day. A pattern is developing here, and every day I wonder what my eyes will encounter upon opening. I imagine, in my childlike recesses, new adventures, surprise happenstances of imminent history, and more—all of these elements swirl about me like fine wine in a crystal glass of timeless implication.

In a complete about-face to my here-to-for mentioned youthful exuberance, I find I suffer a complete lack of motivation to get up and out into this particular day's stuff and substance. Something is holding me back from the desire to become a part of it—I deem it to be the early hour and pull the pillow over my head. That accomplishes nothing, and I conclude that by opening my eyes one at a time I won't commit to the day too quickly. Finally, I opt for the eye closest to the window, hoping to find something there. I see nothing that appears out of the ordinary and am disappointed by my expectations. The other eye follows suit and nothing has changed.

Still, Hurricane Hills has grown on me and something is pulling at me to get up and venture out into its offerings. I take my towel and soap to the bathroom at the end of the hall, which is actually just outside my door. If I don't take a bath soon there will be other things growing on me besides the town. And the enjoyment and comfort I derive from cold water, a cramped, stained, rusted claw-foot tub and kerosene-smelling soap with the texture of industrial grade sandpaper is greater than I ever could have imagined.

After a bathing experience that borders on extreme sports, followed by embellishing seen and unseen surfaces with aromatics, I return to my room and add minimal apparel to my sorry frame. Then I make my way down a now familiar hallway to the lobby. I try not to look toward the registration desk but sneak a glance in its direction. Just as I feared, she is standing there almost frozen in her personal time. This is getting very waxy and I feel like I am already having a very bad "her" day. I ignore her and move on into an unknown mission.

I stumble through the front doors and out onto the boardwalk. My momentum carries me off its splintery edge and into the middle of a dusty street. Staring down the bygone avenue's imaginary centerline, I become lost in its absence. I fall to my knees in the middle of the street and press my face into the soil. Suddenly, out of nowhere, horses and old cars are swerving to avoid me, though, oddly, the drivers are looking straight ahead as if I am not there. The sidewalks are streaming with people. Especially noticeable are the ladies and their long, flowing, dresses adorned with colors, frills, and sashes as they carry parasols draped in ribbons that dance in the wind. One of us is not really here. I haven't determined if it's them or me. I try to gain control of what is going on, but with my head in the dust and the hot sun on my back, I freeze. I now know why I was apprehensive about entering into this day. God called this meeting and has me in a position where He can now get my attention. The people around me are the dancers, players, and extras on the set whereupon I have taken center stage. I have an audience, but not the one I am seeing in the fringes. I have an audience with God, and I must applaud the creativity in his choice of venues.

With my face in the dirt and my heart in His hands, I cry into the nadir of the waiting soil. It occurs to me now that I didn't roll out of the sack this morning, nonchalantly decide to mosey downstairs, and leisurely stroll along a shaded avenue on my way to a hot latte. I was jerked from my bed, given a cold-water baptism, and thrown out into the street by the Man because He had some business to address with His child.

As soon as I hit the dirt I knew I needed to bow down and worship, and that is just what I am doing. I find I have to bury my head almost all the way into a rut in the road to get down enough to qualify for pure subservience and devotion. Even this is not sufficient, so I roll over on my back, look to the heavens, and plead revelation. Silence surrounds me while the sound of distant activity continues around the edges, echoing up and down the street. I struggle, unsure of what is being asked of me. I know He loves it when we come before Him with a childlike nature. Because I am on my back, I decide to spread my arms and legs and begin making a dust angel. It is apparent that my actions are not quite nailing it, so I get up, dust myself off and race down the elongated street like a jack-rabbit Jonah trying to get away until I am finally exhausted. To be honest, I am tired of both the exercise and myself. By now the crowd has multiplied, a mixed chorus of boos and encouragement fills the whole town. After all the "escaping," I am still center stage. I stop in my tracks and realize I am totally disoriented and have ended right back where I started—in that same old rut. I have not only lost my earthly senses, but in my fatigue have finally let go. It is in that weakened instance He speaks to me. At the very moment I let down my guard, revelation fills my pores and I realize I have been doing this dance all by myself. In the busyness of my frantic motions, I have completely forgotten Who is in charge. I can only bow out of center stage by exiting my personal performance and entering into the center of His will.

I return to my best idea of the day so far, which is to lie face-down in the dirt and get lost in fervent repentant seeking prayer. I am truly at the end of the road and myself. Once I let go and become buried in my nothingness He comes to me—not like roaring thunder or a turbulent prairie wind, not in eagles screeching over-head, but in a Holy moment when all things subside and meld into silence. It is at this point He says, "Be still my child and let Me soothe your soul, let Me calm your disquiet—let Me show the way." Scriptures and prom-ises come crashing down on me in recognition of His essence and sweet purity. He is a simple God, an unas-suming Savior. He is what we long for—truth, peace, and serenity. He is the All...the Ever...the One.

"You are drifting." He speaks again, "And that is okay; as long as you keep your eyes on Me you are moving in the right direction." I can feel Him drawing very close to me in this moment. He then kneels down beside me. One hand rests on my shoulder, and with the other He writes in the dust. This little encounter is a simple gut-check to make sure I am not wandering away but pressing in at all times no matter where I roam and what I see. I know now I am to enter in and never slip away from His Holy purpose for my existence. There is no condemnation in the moment—only a sweet fragrance of love and forgiveness.

Then it is over...

I stand up and look at the crowd around me. They simultaneously turn away and slowly dissolve as they leave the scene of my grime. I look down at my feet and have to catch my breath. There on the ground are two dust angels in the road. I head back toward the hotel with the feeling that God just wrestled me to the ground. Something important happened back there at the end of the street, and I am sure it all had to with my walk—that is when I notice I am limping.

As I evolve back to earthen reality, I reach up and feel the drool on my face that has blended with the dirt from the soil I was pressed into—this could be the very reason everyone disappeared. I find strange comfort in knowing that when I get to the hotel the clerk will remain poised as always and will not notice me, much less give me a strange look.

I cover the ground between this bewildering encounter and my hotel with no awareness of how I have made the transition. I was wrong about the clerk. As I enter the lobby and move quickly toward the stairs, I glance sideways. As expected, there she is calicoed and comatose except for her own sideways glance at my face. Like an Annie Oakley of the Hiltons, she smiles demurely and raises her hand slightly, pointing to the side of her mouth to indicate the muddened drool coming from mine. At that moment I decide I like her better without a personality. I give her a disdainful grunt and run up the stairs to my room and grab my towel and soap, retreating to the sink in the bathroom where I splash cold water on my face. As my hands slide from my forehead to my chin, it feels like an unveiling. I look into the mirror and see myself for the first time. He called me child out there on the road, and with childlike innocence I can feel myself assembling the pieces of my being—putting them together like broken and discarded toys of time. I see a bit of everyone I've met on this journey in my reflection, and the lines of my face are not clearly defined. They are rounded off, smoothed out, and accented by shadows and the makeup of each person's touch on my life during this journey. This moment and His words speak of disclosure and a peaceful calm comes over me. I return to my room to wait.

I disrobe and crawl into bed completely drained and close my eyes one at a time, reversing how I began the day. My breathing becomes electric and conjures shades of unheard melodies; the ceiling fan overhead sorts out unknown rhythms from undiscovered places. I think back to what just happened and realize I like the person I just met in a broken mirror, in a second floor bathroom…at the end of an empty hall.

Platinum laced rain falls silently outside the wonder window in my room. I fade back into the dream that began dreaming me when I first set out on this mysterious journey…

An old man holding a fiddle in one hand and a dusty bow in the other appears in my dream. He leads me to a grove of trees in a meadow and motions for me to sit on the ground at the base of a large rock. He sits before me and begins to play a song that embraces all the music of the centuries—a single song, a simple song, a song of life. I watch him in silhouette as he plays. He leans into the instrument—which sounds more like a soaring lute—eyes closed, long hair gracing the edges of his face. All the rhythms of the people I met on this journey lock into one flowing and pulsating cadence. The low sun in the sky creates a halo effect along the edges. It is then that I notice his hands. They are exactly like the hands of the other men in my dreams, except this time they are not covering each other, and for the first time I can see them clearly. A long wide scar travels from the center, front and back of each hand, to the base of his fingers, interrupting and accenting their sinewy strength and delicate lines. His name is David and he sings me a story. I can see and feel it as it unfolds before me. It has a soundtrack. The music fades and his song evolves into words. From the distant background I hear muted drums in prelude...

DOKA CHIGA...DOKA CHIGA...DOKA CHIGA...
DOKA CHIGA...DOKA CHIGA...

18

THREE CHORDS & AN ATTITUDE

[DAVID]

DOKA CHIGA…DOKA CHIGA…DOKA CHIGA…
DOKA CHIGA…DOKA CHIGA…

"JOSEPH HAD A PROBLEM HOLDING still when he was a child. His hands were always moving. His fingers flew, probing the air, and were always clattering across things. He loved exploring the elements, mainly for their rhythm and the sound they would make when he pounded on them. His attention would fall to an odd-shaped item or a group of similar objects. From this point of childlike observance, he would further examine their shapes and resonances, finally engaging them in patterned clamor and bang. As time evolved, things became a little more organized and the objects of his deflections became more musical and specific. The rhythms tightened, fluidity developed, and cadence melded into the semblance of something almost perceptible…acceptable even.

"He was attracted to the washing machine and often could be found lying on the floor with his back pressed up tight to it while it was going through its gyrations. Because his was a big family, that old washer chugged most of the day and night. They were poor, and every night each child had to scramble to find a place to sleep. The formal sleeping spots were usually reserved for the youngest and the oldest of their cluttered coterie, bedrooms being limited to parents and newborns. A full dirty-clothes-basket was considered a score for the night and served as protection from a hard floor. So he slept and studied there, watching the cold January nights perched on top of the warm washer. As it churned in perfect tempo, he would dream in distant time signatures while looking out through the small icy window above the washer's controls into the country night.

GADA BAHCHUNK…GADA BAHCHUNK…
GADA BAHCHUNK…GADA BAHCHUNK…

"School was extremely difficult because he was supposed to sit still. The problem was something inside his head was always moving something outside his body. He was held back and unable to move forward because of a beckoning backbeat. For him, 4/4 was a time signature he kept track of with his tapping toes, not a whole-number fraction. Classmates found him to be aloof because of his detached countenance and they found his faraway gaze disconcerting. As a result, he got into lots of scraps after school, though even his punches found a tempo.

CATUNGA CA CHUNK…CATUNGA CA CHUNK…
CATUNGA CA CHUNK…CATUNGA CA CHUNK…

"As he grew up, all this stuff started bubbling from beneath the surface and something had to give. No musical instrument was off limits to his inquiring hands and heart. He was a dotted accent waiting to happen. In the near distance was Kathleen, a waiting calm in his rising storm, watching quietly, knowing there would be a time to enter his song. She didn't know she knew this; she was a child too. But in time, a different rhythm entered their lives as they discovered each other—drawn together as if by divine appointment, falling in silent step on their long walks to school from their distant homes. In these almost wordless times together over the years, they grew into a deep understanding, an effortless transformation into an unspoken bond.

"Then, out of nowhere, the local Elks Club—in Joseph's rural Americana where everyone wore a lot of blue and starched white—got a call that Duke Ellington's band needed a place to land between gigs and pick up some extra change as they made their long way from one engagement to another. The vast plains and scrublands of his small town lay strategically in between these two points. A new tint was on its way into the local color. Because he washed the store-front windows outside the downtown Elks Club once a week (in addition to his after school cleanup duties in the card room, which doubled as the dance hall on special occasions), he got to hang around that night until the show was over. In exchange, he would lend his expertise to the late-night task of cleaning up cigarette butts, spilled drink stains, and wiping down the worn chairs and tables.

"There was a spot at the bottom of the stage riser, just to the right of the piano, that was inaccessible to the patrons, used to store the bands' instrument cases and hide the cables. He sensed something was going to happen that night, so he reported for duty early. Minutes before the show began he curled up in the hollow of a base drum case in that darkened alcove for a close up view of what was to come. The band came out and, to his wonder, he could see up under the front-right leg of the piano directly into the face of the Duke himself. Then, out of the periphery and through the smoke, another amazing man stepped up to the microphone and was introduced as Joe Williams. Here's where a twelve-year-old backwoods boy felt his heart stop and race simultaneously through the swelling of a deep Blues groove. There was something about these black dudes and the way they moved—the way they closed their eyes, sang, played their instruments, and set things in motion. It was, for our young hero, what you might call black magic. It was incomprehensible; it was something unimagined, yet strangely longed for. Phonic fantasies and decibel dreams emerged and then merged into his very being that night. Looking back, it was like being launched in a rocket ship as your first experience in velocity.

"BAH DOOM SHA BOOMP...BAH DOOM SHA BOOMP... BAH DOOM SHA BOOMP...

"This young man with an unidentified dream and a heart beating for music was discovering one of its supreme forms at an early age. A point of transformation was lodged into the deep of Joseph's being. For many years he had done the things expected of a young man with common beginnings rather than what was in his heart—a heart that pounded with a myriad of time signatures. He crawled into a small space beneath the bandstand that night; but, he knew someday he was going to emerge from this secluded space like a butterfly out of a cocoon into something beautiful—something that would fly wide and color deep into an unfamiliar fabric beyond his comprehension. You cannot put your finger on that certain something, but you have to credit God for His abundance in giving glorious gifts of unusual abilities to the most unlikely people. For two hours at a small town Elks club, seeds were being planted that would yield a harmonic harvest to come.

"That night in the bass drum case changed everything. Kathleen noticed a difference in Joseph the next day—who now insisted on being called 'Joe' just like the big black man with the smoky-blue voice. Kathleen was his rock, she was home, she was always the unwavering quiet is his storm. While he was bouncing off the walls, she was holding steady in faithful countenance. It was almost as if he could only come down to Earth to land in her warm arms—arms that would hold and calm him down.

"They had always known each other. They were next-door neighbors even though their houses were over a quarter-mile apart. Kathleen was content with the smell and feel of the trees and grasses surrounding their houses, and, at nineteen, had never been more than nine miles from home. She was indeed beautiful, but her true beauty resided within—a humility and personal peace that didn't need to be anywhere other than this quiet place. Her lithe figure, graced by long flowing honey-tinged hair, seemed to move in concert with the wind. Long eyelashes shaded and protected a steady, kind, and almost winsome look that poured forth from her delicate face. There was a gentle composure in all her movements and expressions. She was more than an occupant of this tranquil setting—she was an integral part.

"Joe, by contrast, had a nervous energy that made him appear to be moving even when he was standing still. Even though this was a time before there were rock stars, Joe looked like…a rock star. Long lean legs supporting a sinewy body—strong arms that embraced his instruments to the degree that there was no space between them when he engaged them in song. He wore his dark, shiny hair long like the natives of the local tribe. His eyes were green as the grasses of the surrounding fields and it was as if he had a switch with only two settings that he used to control them. When he was in Kathleen's world they had the softness of brookside moss, privately inviting to those he trusted and held dear. When he was performing they darkened; they flashed and flared, darting and penetrating the depth of everything with in his field of vision. People used to joke that when Joe was playing music he stood tall even if he was in a hole. Even though they were as opposite as the east and the west, Joe and Kathleen were joined at the heart in this, the place they called home.

"They were united in the soul-building process of the growing years, sharing the simplicity of being brought up country. It was not a matter of discussion but a sense of the natural that they would always be together. They were wordless in this communication, sharing an unexplainable bond that held them together no matter where they were. A small, rolling indentation in the fields between their houses that did not quite qualify as a canyon—in those days some folks called them hollows or hollers—created the only distance between them. This one was filled with poplar and cottonwood trees. Temperatures, winds, light, and smells all changed the minute they entered the space. It was as if there were a quiet cathedral caused by an almost perfect circular mini-meadow in its very center anchored by a smooth sloping rock shaped like a huge chaise lounge for two. They would sit on the ground, lean back against its curved slope and look up through the trees at a clear sky. The mid-day sun would heat its smooth surface, and when dusk approached they would meet there and the rock kept them warm. Joe would become settled here in this private space while she was excited by the beauty and peace of it.

"They often passed the time beneath these trees, dreaming of other worlds and talking about things they wanted to experience someday. There were the big unimaginable things—private jets, cruising on a yacht, lunch with Frank Sinatra, dancing at the White House—fantasies they knew would never come true. Then there were the real wishes, the simplicity of which was alive with possibility because these dreams could come true, and that awareness filled their hearts with the excitement of anticipation.

"'Joe,' Kathleen would ask, her tempo almost adagio-like, the words flowing smoothly into the warm air, 'wouldn't it be great if we could bring all our fantasies and dreams into this place and enjoy it all here?'

"Joe's answer, by contrast, came forth in a staccato, measured reflection. Although in direct opposition to her interpretation of their united dream, his response was in no way argumentative. It was the same dream approached from a different angle.

"'Yeah, or how about loading all this beauty onto our private yacht and taking it with us to Rio De Janeiro for Mardi Gras and have all the great Brazilian musicians play their best music just for us in our transported meadow?'

"Then they both would grow silent, gazing skyward while resting in the shared comfort of their central theme—being together and loving how they felt lying side by side in this space. To observe their faces in these moments, it would seem as though she was in worship and he was amid creation of melodies for an unwritten song.

"Kathleen was a great baker. She often prepared white cakes, her favorite dessert, for others when they celebrated special occasions, though no one had ever thought to bake an all-white cake for her birthday or special occasion. She dreamed of having multiple white cakes on her wedding day—their wedding day—the most special occasion she could imagine…in their tree lined meadow sanctuary.

"Joe often complained that because he was the most accomplished musician in their remote area, he provided the music for every barn raising, school dance, and harvest moon party. None of the other local musicians were willing to play for these special occasions, so he usually ended up playing them with his band. Instead of being able to dance or enjoy the party, he had to play, set up, and do the tear down for the events. As much as he loved music, Joe felt trapped, especially when it came to the proms and New Year's Eve celebrations. He was unable to have a social life because he had to work all night while all the other kids were having a good time. He assumed that in the future he would probably be playing mostly during weekends and holidays; but that was different—it was an occupation, a calling, and a goal—and this was now.

"He dreamed that someday great musicians would play just for him at his most joyful event: the day he and Kathleen married. They laughed at the absurdity of the dreams filled with mansions and servants, but they believed the real desires of their hearts would be fulfilled someday. However, it was here as he looked up at the sky that he dreamed about leaving, while it was here that she dreamed they would settle and never leave. She had everything she ever needed when she laid here next to Joseph, and she didn't really care about what she did not know. He was drawn into the possibilities of the unknown and wanted what he didn't even realize he did not have. As odd as it seemed, it was this difference that tied them together and was only comprehensible to them.

"It wasn't as if they didn't talk about these things, because they did. Their verbal explorations existed in that space between those two dichotomies. The glue that held most of their musings in place was based on an ancient tradition followed by the local Indian tribe as part of their most sacred rituals, using the nuance of trinity as their center point.

"If a member of their Indian nation was suspected of a misdeed, a friend, parent, or elder could ask them point-blank if they had committed this particular offense. It was not considered bad or dishonest for the accused to be misleading in answering the charge when it was presented the first time (the white man's white lie?), nor would it be considered an insult on the part of the inquiring party for asking that first time. For the accuser to bring the question of impropriety forward a second time was approaching accusation, challenge, and potential disrespect. For the accused to lie the second time was of equal significance. Both parties, at this point—one bordering on insult and the other possibly a falsehood—were now walking on shaky ground. This is usually where the encounter ceased and some resolution was sought because taking it to the next step was a very serious matter. For the accuser to persist, asking the question a third time, was a full-blown confrontation, and carried life and death consequences. To deny a third time, if the denial was a lie, placed the culprit in the very arms of the wrath of the Great Spirit. Neither party could complete the third round without one of them being dead wrong.

"As serious as this traditional exchange was, it could also be used in less dire circumstances—a marriage ceremony, for example, where the equivalent of 'Do you promise to love, honor, and obey?' was asked of each person before saying their wedding vows. Answering yes to the question three times represented an irrevocable lifetime commitment, and, if broken, moved the offender back into the line of fire for the wrath of God.

"Joe and Kathleen used this practice in the middle ground where most of their conversations dwelled and treated it as a loving gesture. If they ran out of understanding or agreement, or if going to the third question was out of bounds, each could sense at what point to bow out of the dialogue. This arrangement was not one of negotiation but of a deep understanding developed through their union. Sometimes they would play with this solemn tradition…

"'Joe,' Kathleen would ask, staring intently into his eyes, 'Do you love me?'

"Joe would answer her with a fixed stare, 'Yes I do my love.'

"'Then play me a song,' she would reply with a smile.

"Without breaking stride or stance Joe would say, 'Kathleen, do you love me?'

"'Yes I do Maestro,' she would reply assuredly and even a bit demurely.

"'Then bake me a cake,' would become his immediate and stock answer.

"Instead of getting more serious as they moved into the second phase, their tone brightened and their smiles lightened as they repeated both the questions and the answers exactly as they had done the first time. The third time they would leave the ancient pattern, grasp the other's outstretched hands and say together. 'Do you love me?'

"Looking into each other's eyes, they would quietly affirm their commitment in unison…'You know I do.'

"It was an innocent, renewal of vows between two unquestioning young lovers.

"Kathleen believed in Jesus with all of her being and would see Him through the soft mist as she looked up at the sky. She could feel Him in the morning air she breathed when walking into this special place. She could hear His words in the winds caressing the trees encircling her as she came to rest on the rock.

"Joe couldn't care less, but felt a certain comfort in her faith and never questioned her. He had no problem joining her when asked to be a part of her journey. But, deep down, he only believed in things that had a backbeat and a tag ending. It wasn't real unless he could hear it or feel it in his being. One day he left their gentle spot beneath the cottonwoods and poplars. There was not the warm, close discussion they usually had when it came to sharing their deepest feelings.

"He simply said, 'Kathleen, I'm leaving.'

"He assured her in the midst of this sudden (yet oddly expected) exit that one-day he would return. They both knew she would be there despite how unfair the arrangement seemed. They hugged and said, 'I love you,' three times, and after the third time he was gone.

"There was a moment, an unknown point in time, where Joe's history moved to a different place. It was about the music, the soul, the drive, and the intensity of the creative force that enters a chosen few who have worked something special into their being without even realizing it. Joe had spent years working on his fingers and their relation to flow and tempo, the hand-eye coordination, the beat that lies within being melded to the melody that flows above. But, there is nothing like the astonishment that comes in the incredible moment when suddenly the head, hands, and heart become one—when what you feel, what you hear, and what you want to do all comes together as one magical sonic entity.

"His new awareness made him realize he was no longer subject to the tangible, but instead had become strangely cognizant of what he had been gathering from the periphery. His time had come.

"Joe pulled together a band of the best musicians from the surrounding counties and named it the Ben Jammins. Benjamin was his younger brother and, outside of Kathleen, was the only one he felt would never betray him. Young Ben idolized Joe and sat at his feet for hours as he practiced his instruments. Also, Ben would listen intently to the music that shaped Joe's understanding. Joe vowed that when he became famous he would take care of Ben.

LONG YEARS, MANY MILES, AND A MILLION MOMENTS LATER

"The Ben Jammins were a force from the get-go. They were a tight-knit bunch of talented musicians; and, not only were they successful, they became a real band of brothers. It was almost hard to look back and remember the garage band years, the freebie gigs, the auditions, the rejections, the band fights, the crooked promoters, the constant hunger, the cheap-shot artists, and the backstabbers. Immense fame acts almost like a narcotic, a sedative, and a deadening knockout punch, all at once disengaging the bad times that preceded the good. Joe endured endless hard miles on not-so-friendly roads. Smelly hotel rooms, eternal bad food, bunking down with five guys in a crash pad that would be vacated when the rent came due, sleeping in the back of the road van between the equipment cases became merely vague remembrances. Suites and sweets replaced the sweats and smells of the roads traveled to get to this exhilarating moment of grand success. His heart and hands never stopped beating out a pattern that was bound to lead to success. Dogged determination had been replaced by fabulous fame.

"In the early years, Joe returned home often, knowing Kathleen would always be there. This constancy, coupled with the unchanging landscape of their youth, kept them united in spirit. As his fame and wealth grew, as well as its importance in his life, he needed her 'ways' less. During this same passage of time, her walk in God's way grew deeper and deeper. It would seem that this would drive them apart; but, for some strange reason, it drew them closer. She often prayed for him and for his safe return.

"Joe became absorbed by his success and took full advantage of its offerings, delving deeper and deeper into the drug world that surrounded the phenomenon of fame. As his decadence and dependence on chemical stimulation grew, so did his despondency. Something was missing in the midst of it all. Paranoia often becomes a natural companion to those who adopt this exaggerated lifestyle. In time, he developed an odd vision of his demise. In the midst of all the fancy living and good times, it didn't make sense that he was becoming preoccupied with his death; but, he kept envisioning a day when he would walk out on a stage, look down to a specific spot beneath him, and recognize a floor he had seen in his dreams. In each dream, when he came to the precise place he saw so many times, he would die there. The reason for his death was always different, and the floor was never in the same building or town, which prevented him from seeing it coming. The only thing he recognized was the floor itself, and then it would be too late because he would already be there. The floor and its appearance were the only constants—there were no other clues he could take into real life.

"He would break into a cold sweat each time the visions came to him, and they began happening more frequently. His déjà vu began kicking in almost every time the band went on stage. It was easy to hide this feeling from the Ben Jammins because the crowds were getting larger, the auditoriums bigger, and could be chalked up to pre-concert jitters. He never shared this premonition with the band or Kathleen. In fact, he shared less and less with her. When he did think about her, he visualized her life as it had always been. However, years had passed and his detachment blinded him to the fact that things were not the same back home.

"Kathleen's mother had passed away, and even without Joe in her life, she managed to get by, but things got tough when her father also died. She and Ben developed a special bond during this time; so, when Joe's family moved away, everyone agreed it would be best that Ben remain with her to be raised since Joe would most likely return there during breaks from the road. What little inheritance she received was eventually gone, and the reality was that there was no work to be had without moving away. Joe's folks were able to help some; but it was not enough to sustain them, and she found herself in a situation she never thought she would have to face. She knew of Joe's wealth; but, country pride would never allow her to ask for help until one day she was no longer able to feed Ben. She called Joe and shared her current circumstances with him. He insisted they come live with him, vowing that the place they had grown up in would be preserved for their eventual return. He would have his accountants, managers, agents, publicists, bookers, personal trainers, and roadies see to everything.

"She had grown to love Ben and did the one thing she never dreamed she would do—leave home and join

Joe's world—in order to provide for him. Food was back on the table, but caring for Ben and time alone with the Word and God's love became her only other sustenance. Joe was usually gone on the road or 'gone' when he was home.

"His repeated promise to her was that when the next tour and album were finished he would, hang it all up and take her home again.

"He even made an acoustic recording of the old song 'I'll Take You Home Again, Kathleen' so she could play this promise to fall asleep to while he was gone on the road.

"He was in Albuquerque when he got the devastating news: Someone had broken into the house looking for drugs and Kathleen was shot in the back when she shielded Ben. By the time Joe was able to book a private plane and make his way to the hospital, the news concerning Kathleen's condition was not good. When he arrived at the nurse's station on her floor he was told she was so heavily sedated they would not be able to communicate, and the next few hours would be devoted to trying to keep her alive. He could go home or wait at the hospital, but the itinerary for this venue was very clear-cut. It was going to be touch and go and the surgery scheduled for the following morning would be a matter of life and death.

"Joe decided to stay, wanting to be close to her once again. He eventually fell asleep straddled across two chairs in the waiting room. When he awoke, he was told that she had just been taken into surgery. It would be several hours before there was any indication of the eventual outcome. He waited around for a while and then finally drove home in a state of disbelief. He began having a change of heart about the life he had chosen and decided he also needed a change of clothes and a hot shower. He hadn't taken any drugs since he received the news; but, as the driver pulled through the gates of his mansion, he had never felt more stoned or completely out of it. He was almost to the front door when he noticed his band mates' cars in his driveway. He felt comforted because he believed they had come to stand by him at this crucial time. Albuquerque had been the final stop on the tour and they followed his departure by a few hours in the band bus.

"As Joe walked into the grand entry, he could hear them talking in the large study beyond the curved stairway leading to the upstairs rooms. In the giant expanse of his mansion, this room was where Joe really lived, and it was where the band of brothers spent many hours creating music. When Joe walked into the room all conversation stopped and he found himself standing in the center. He felt strangely alone and felt anything but embraced in brotherhood. They were all seated on the massive couches and chairs that filled the library end of the room. The Ben Jammins looked away one by one as he scanned their familiar faces. Soon he was staring at the tops of heads as they looked to the floor. They had not come to comfort him but to tell him they were brothers no more. They felt his ego, excesses, and personal crises were too much to handle. They shuffled and stuttered in low disjointed tones and sentence fragments; but, the message was simple—they were abandoning him and sat wordless as the management team, and the professional entourage of accountants and lawyers they'd amassed around their enterprise, in very formal fashion, laid out his generous 'severance package' as they gave him the boot from the band he founded—cutting him out of the music that was his life.

"A very long day without drugs, a sudden betrayal, and Kathleen's tragedy left Joe frozen. One by one, the band of brothers got up and walked silently past him as they made their way to the door and out of his life. Years of struggling arm in arm, walking the hard road of a tough business hand in hand, ended with a weak hug and a shaky, 'See ya, bro.'

"Joe had never cried himself to sleep before, but his face was still wet when he woke to the phone ringing across the room. He was dazed and exhausted as he lay on the couch, still wearing the clothes he had from two days ago. The call was from Ben: 'I'm at the hospital, call me when you get here and I'll meet you in the lobby. I love you.'

"Ben and the nurse in charge met Joe at the elevator. He was told the operation's outcome was iffy and that the prognosis was not good. They were taken to the resident chief surgeon's office, and from there they were ushered into a private lounge to await results. The minute they walked in, Joe looked down at the floor and tears flooded his eyes, pouring out from every fiber and lonely broken place inside his being. There was the floor—that floor—the one in his dreams. It was supposed to be a stage floor in a giant concert hall, not a waiting room in a smelly hospital. He fell to his knees on its scuffed surface and prayed. This was the floor he was to die on—but it wasn't to be from bullets or fire— it was the place he was to die to self and be born again. Everything that Kathleen had ever told him about Jesus and faith and healing and forgiveness and redemption and love and mercy and grace washed over him—intro, verse, bridge, and chorus. His crying was no longer about his loss, but had turned into crying out to God to save his soul and Kathleen's life.

"Lord please let me take her home to the country again, he prayed.

"The doctor came to the door and knocked softly before entering. Because Joe was so anxious to hear what the doctor had to say, the time it took him to utter his first words felt longer than any international flight Joe had ever taken. It was good news and bad news: she was going to make it but would be permanently paralyzed from the waist down. He told Joe she should awaken in about six hours, so he should take Ben to get something to eat, and then go home to freshen up. Hospital recovery and therapy would take a few months and everything—schedules, priorities, home life—would all require revaluation.

"They walked out into a cold winter night. Joe put Ben in the waiting limo and asked him to wait a minute. He walked across the parking lot into a small grassy area in a park that bordered the hospital complex and knelt once more, alone in the dark. He reaffirmed the earlier deal he had made with God—his first prayer. This time he did not need a manager or agent to authorize the agreement. The deal he made on the floor in the doctor's office would be honored from this point on, and the accomplishments and bounties of his entire life would be shared with Kathleen in her time of need. It was then he realized that Ben had come from the car and was kneeling beside him. Ben had learned about the Lord at Kathleen's table over the many years they had spent together. He was joining Joe in agreement as they made their requests known before the Father.

"Over the following months Joe spent all of his time either at Kathleen's side or with Ben restoring their two homes in the country to their original beauty in order to get everything ready for her return. Joe had been too stoned and too distant over the years to notice that Ben had grown into a fine young man, a gentle man. He was a man with Kathleen's sensibilities and love for simple honest things. Joe sold his mansion almost immediately after the night of the Ben Jammin's breakup and easily had the financial means to move the two houses together so they could be combined as one. But, Joe didn't just move one next to the other; he had them both positioned to face the opening through the trees that surrounded the shadowed glen where they had spent so much precious time together.

"The place was finally ready, and the day came for Joe to pick up Kathleen from the hospital. She and Joe had picked out a beautiful white outfit for her to wear home. The tragedy had brought scattered families and old friends back together, and a couple of the ladies from the reunited clan came to the hospital early to help Kathleen get dressed and ready for the trip home. She looked like an angel. Besides fixing up the old homestead during her long stay and recovery at the hospital Joe had also been able to restore the relationship with the band of brothers and they were now closer than ever. Joe was actually grateful to them because their 'selling him out' had actually 'bought him' a better life.

"Joe purchased the old band bus from the Ben Jammins to transport Kathleen home. He had removed all the bunks from the back, replacing them with a custom lounge for Kathleen to lie on. It was positioned so she could look out the window and see the outside world once again as they left some bad memories behind. The old rock and roll interior had been modified to a softer and more feminine style—swaths of white material replacing a lot of brown leather. The hospital was only four hours away from their destination, and the ride was a smooth one filled with close friends, continuous laughter, and great stories about the place of their youth: a place called home.

"The bus pulled up to the edge of a wheat field on a section of the family property, the airbrakes swooshed, announcing their arrival. The band's long-time driver of that old bus gently picked up Kathleen and carried her out of the bus and placed her in Joe's open and waiting arms. He and Joe exchanged glances—this wasn't the first time he'd had to carry someone off that bus. They both knew that this time was the last and there was purpose: the end of a long road.

"Joe carried her in his arms straight from the field to the grove and across a flower-strewn threshold into the grassy center of the poplars and pines where they used to dream their dreams of special things to come. As they entered the cathedral of their youth, the Ben Jammins were singing 'I'll Take You Home Again, Kathleen.'

"Relatives and loved ones from many miles and many years had been brought together in celebration and love as they welcomed Joseph and Kathleen home. Holding hands, they formed an inner circle within the circle of trees that were nature's cathedral. They joined in the song. It was a circle that would never again be broken.

"Joseph gently placed her on a velvet pillow with her back leaning on the warm rock foundation of their youth. While she watched, he picked a bouquet of wild flowers from the glen. He presented himself before her, knelt, placed the flowers in her hands, and asked her to marry him. She looked over Joseph's shoulder and saw

Pastor Stone who had brought Kathleen up in the Lord's teaching. He was standing in front of them and the rock where they used to lie many years ago planning the day they would be married. She said, 'Yes, of course. Everything I have ever loved surrounds me in this place.'

"Joseph sat down beside her and leaning back, they looked into the sky through the cathedral canopy. Pastor Stone knelt before them, opened his Bible, and presented their marriage vows. He then stood up and asked them to close their eyes for the final part of the ceremony:

'Joseph, do you love Kathleen?'

'Yes.'

'Then keep her in your care.'

'Kathleen, do you love Joseph?'

'Yes.'

'Then keep him in your heart.'

'Joseph, do you love Kathleen?'

'Yes.'

'Then surround her with your faith.'

'Kathleen, do you love Joseph?'

'Yes.'

'Then give yourself completely.'

"The Pastor paused before asking the third time…

'Joseph, do you love Kathleen?'

'Yes.'

'Kathleen, do you love Joseph?'

'Yes.'

'Then stop shaking and kiss each other!'

"When they opened their eyes, after the world's longest kiss, the sun had gone behind the trees casting shadows over the meadow, causing it to be bathed in a soft warm dusk. During the last part of the ceremony, dozens of women from around the county had quietly entered and circled the edges of the cathedral and then lit hundreds of candles on white cakes, giving a halo effect to the glen. A lifelong wish had just come true—this was that most beautiful moment and she knew in her heart that it was worth the wait. So many tears over so many years, and now they glistened in the candlelight as they ran down her smiling face.

"It had been a long time since Joseph had cried tears of joy, but when he realized that practically every great musician he had ever admired and played with over the years came into the meadow through the trees singing and playing for just him and his bride, he totally lost it and began weeping with joy. He threw his head back and just listened…no one invited him to play.

"Kathleen was home again and Joseph's head, hands, and heart had come to rest…to a single song, a simple song, a song of life."

DOKA CHIGA…DOKA CHIGA…DOKA CHIGA…
DOKA CHIGA…DOKA…

19

EXODUST

[PHILCO]

I HAD JUST BEEN LOOKING into the sky enjoying the luxuriant calm of a tree-lined, candlelit cathedral; but, I have come to discover that when I become overwhelmed with the richness of God's beauty and the way He moves, I tend to move with Him. The music of the meadow fades into the distance...and I slide away to this other place—a faraway land both in distance and time.

This must be the desert.

I feel now as though I have left a magnificent dream and landed somewhere between Fresno and Istanbul. I know that where I am in this moment has to do with where I have been. Somehow I know that everything that has gone before is in me and this place...now.

There is a slight chill in the warm air; my coat is colorful, open at the neck, and I am facing east. I hear the soft sound of muted tinkling bells and a gentle wind slapping the flaps of nomadic tents almost out of sight, off to my right. Far off in the distance and slightly to my left I can see a cluster of olive trees. The wind follows my vision to that distant grove and returns with the sweet scent of the fallen fruit as it ripens on sacred ground.

I stand on the edge of an arid region. It is different from my homeland and very different from the luxuriant enclosure I emerged from just seconds before. There is incredible meaning to this ground, and the feet that have walked upon it have left deep impressions. Their sound is what has drawn me here and still echoes in the wind as it passes by me on its way into eternity. Firm foundations were laid upon this soil that offered little in apparent worth to so many who traveled upon its import; yet, over time its significance demands respect for its history and purpose. I am tied to this place even though I have never been here. It mysteriously pulls at a part of me I have no right to claim, other than dwelling in its existent stages. I am in a new state…of mind and location.

It is at this point I realize we have sold ourselves into slavery. The brothers of origin that shaped our lives have betrayed us. We have dug our own pit and rejected the lessons to be learned from wallowing in its mire; but, God knows us, and He knows our hearts. He has written a beautiful song for us to sing and is patiently waiting for a ragged band to once again emerge from the deep and tune up. The music we are to make is of our own creation; but the libretto is of His design. The postlude to a long melodious journey crescendos across the sandy expanse that surrounds this moment and melds into the quietude of the morning air. The drifting ceases to be random and has gathered distant focus.

The wind returns to my view and brings with it the melodics that were made and the lyrics written during a time I remember with both fondness and lament. As vast as the area encompassing this errant manifestation appears to be, I am curiously filled with the sensation of being released from captivity. From the cramped quarters of this reflection, scenes from another time come into focus and I sense it will only take one more step to walk away into complete freedom. It is a step of faith that will finally deliver me—a walk with God and a waiting in obedience that will allow me to bless those who were of my roots and my soul.

I begin walking away from all the tangible items that fall within my range of vision. I head toward the only place that has no definition—a place I could not see when

I was observing the obvious things before me. The longer I walk away from this point of formation the closer it appears I am coming upon somewhere special. The level of silence is turned up to ten and soon there is complete sensorial nothingness, leaving only thoughts to feed me, memories to shelter me, and forgotten regrets that once accused me. I know I am being led, and completion is somewhere in the mix of this motion.

The journey is closing in on itself. I am here to understand how I came about, and it is here I find myself, and this is where I am. I smell beginnings here. I can taste time without end in the air. I can feel home so deeply that it raises the hair on the back of my neck. The desert evolves around me as it grows trees, canyons, rivers, and long stretches of green. I can hear the cries that brought me into the world, bouncing off the clouds, and I can smell her warmth as she gave me life. My name is being called and I don't want to be late. It's not a call for coming back...this is about deeply leaving.

I want my mother.

20

WHERE FOREVER BEGINS

[PHILCO]

I PREPARED TO LEAVE HER bedside after touching her for the longest time I can ever remember. She kept my hand in hers the whole time I was there. Holding it faintly yet firmly, this gentle woman looked straight into my eyes; and, with all she had left to offer, climbed into the deepest point of my soul. Then, in the same godly strength she mustered to give me birth, she let me go. With lips barely moving, I heard my mother say, "Keep me inside."

Her name was Marian—Marian Elizabeth.

I had received a call from my dad that the end was near. He said I'd better come while she was still coherent. I knew this was the last time I would ever see her. It is funny how as a child I was always trying to get out of the house and away from my folks so I could do whatever I wanted. Even in my visits during later years my actual time spent were consumed primarily by revisiting the other places and old friends of my growing years instead of just sitting with my loving mom and getting to know her better.

I came to the hospital that morning and the minutes and hours became irrelevant as we talked and remembered things—we never stopped touching each other. Through the traces of age and hard years carved in her face, I once again saw this beautiful young woman of my childhood. I literally had to be torn away from her room as visiting hours came to a close. I wanted more of this wonderful person. She became vibrant and alive in those hours we spent reliving and remembering the past. I so desperately wanted to recapture that which I had never truly grasped.

I was amazed at how special those moments were as we relived the trials, joys, and perils of my youth and her years as a young adult. It was so fascinating looking back on experiences from this twilight perspective. Times and events that were not that much fun in their moment brought smiles and extra touches as we relived them in the warm glow of our shared memories.

Walking away from the old weather-torn brick building that had housed our only hospital for almost a hundred years, I knew deep down I would never see her again. And, on that day, more than a half-century from the day she gave me life, she completed her trilogy as a mother; first, giving birth in a small upstairs bedroom in a backwoods tannery town nestled in a remote valley, followed by sustained prayer for decades until my salvation was secure, and then, finally and lovingly, imparting her beautiful being into my heart as she prepared for her precious peace.

I had debated whether I should fly back to my home or stay there with her while she lingered. The doctor's best estimate of her remaining time was somewhere between two days and two months, so I took a chance and booked my return. On the plane ride back I had a sense of becoming complete as the essence of a mother-child relationship came to fruition in my heart right where she had planted it. She was always a giver and she saved the very best for last. She went right inside of me that day and gave me forever.

Two days later she became clear again and the nurse placed a call for her. We talked over the phone as we had when I was by her side a couple days before. We knew it would be our last conversation even though that fact was unspoken. We said goodbye on the phone, and when I hung up I cried because I wanted my mother.

The next night my father called at three in the morning and said I needed to hurry. He didn't think she was going to last much longer. I was packed and at the airport by 5:00 a.m. trying to get on anything with wings going in that direction. I was resigned to making up an itinerary as I went along. I got a seat on the first plane out of the airport that morning and was on my way home in a matter of minutes.

My dad and younger brother met me at the little hometown airport. Neither said a word or raised their eyes to meet mine as we walked to the car. I knew then that I hadn't made it in time. She left this world before her first-born made it home. We had crossed paths somewhere over Colorado.

With this silent realization ringing in my ears, I walked away from the car and out to the edge of the field in the dry falling dusk. Looking past the small airplane and beyond the barren rolling hills around the landing strip, I could see her in my heart.

I turned to walk back to the car and I could see my dad across the parking lot leaning against a scrawny tree waiting in its meager shade. He was staring eastward as if into a great distance. He and mom had traveled to this place from there a half a century ago to make a new life—a life now as vacant as his stare.

We embrace and he tells me he loves me…for the first time. He takes a piece of paper from his shirt pocket and hands it to me. Looking back at the distance that once surrounded us he speaks again. "Here, son, your mom left you a note."

> *You've come. You knew what to do.*
> *Now you understand—in the deepest part of you,*
> *It is here where it always will be.*
> *It's called home—it cries family.*

A wisp of wind brushed my cheek—a mother's kiss goodbye.

So, this is where forever begins.

21

EVAPORATE

[PHILCO]

I drift back to that rutted road where this journey began;
I am tired…
I look around at that nothingness that has awaited my
return;
I am alone…
I sit down on that rock and try to lean back; but,
I am restless…
I get back up;
I am beckoned…
I fall to my knees;
I am prayer…
I place my face into my palms;
I am worship…

I raise my eyes skyward;
I am uplifted...
I blend with the Wind;
We are One...
I reach for His Word;
It is finished.

I AM BACK FROM WHERE we used to be in our once united state as Americans, and the memories are both invigorating and soothing. We were an exciting country back then because we were made up of our dreams. It was our simplicity, naïveté, and our honest unknowing that made us elegant. Touching once again upon this place has been balm to my soul. I realize now what a gift it is to be able to remember those days and the incredible people that filled their moments.

I am uplifted in spirit because I know our nation still has that same heart and a sound mind. We have a rhythm and flow that is rooted in that long ago and, deep down, we have the soul that does remember what we are about. We are changed, we are ever-changing, yet we're changeless in our uniqueness—all rolled up into a diverse oneness that will see us through and see us back to who we are.

I know now who I am...

I am hard to see when I am leaving. Like evaporation evolving from a fluid beginning—I cling like condensation to a higher place. Eternity engulfs me and I am able to become an integral part of that which is greater than me and meld into the stories about the people who have gone before. I am also in your story, as you are in mine, and together we are in their stories as well. We are all these things because of a book that contains the greatest story ever told. These stories you have been reading here cannot compare with the stories in that book—a special book about eternity that has been prepared by a loving Father for your heart out of love.

I am at rest, seated at the foot of the eternal throne, one hand folded over the other on my left knee. His scarred hands are folded over mine, covering them, holding them for all time. Everything dissipates around me except a warm presence that fills this space. I see the things of life that are real and imagined, past and present, good and bad. I can touch them with my heart, and His Presence surrounds it all.

I am every man.

I feel the sky flash by. I become aware that it is time to come back, not to what lies outside, but what remains within. I experience the sensation of breathtaking motion, and then a knowing that I am being taken to another place—a final home. There is no landing but a sense of brilliant immersion...the sweetness of return. The wind is quiet now and so am I.

This must be Heaven...
I have returned out of ancient entering.
I have entered into a timeless beginning.
Birth, life, and death.
That leaves resurrection...

God bless America—land that I love.

CLOSING NOTE

There is physical beauty to this great land, the people, and their relation to where they are in it is at the heart of it all. It is within this travelogue that I found a special understanding of God and His immense wonderfulness and how He put this all together—Him, us, America, destiny, and these times.

I confess that whenever I walk along our shores, venture into the forests, or gaze across a meadow I sometimes feel that I am among the blessed who truly understand and experience the real adventure, freedom, and romance of this wondrous place. Doctors give us pain pills, evangelists give us hope, the pusher gives us a momentary high, and mothers give us love, while the world gives us nothing. But, God gives us perfection and there is splendor in these surroundings that only the

Master Creator can give. It's perfect because it is free and unconditional like His very nature.

So we come to these places and we find God here. The truth we often fail to realize is the God place we are seeking is actually inside us. We are, in fact, hauling that around with us when we set out in our search of it. For some odd reason we think we have found it when we go somewhere else. He is with us always. That sensation we feel at the seaside, in the pines, or in the middle of a meadow is not a matter of locality; but, for those who understand, it is a covenantal thing. We carry His grandeur within our being. We don't have to book a ticket on the Orient Express to get to it. And, it is beautiful when we have these solitary experiences. Because we are seekers, we have discoveries. Pity the poor souls who look out across the sea and all they see is the investment in the property that it laps upon instead of one of God's many miracles—the warm sand squeezing up between their toes.

It is God we are looking for in these spaces, and it is Him we sense. He is the excitement that is on the very edge of our consciousness that makes it all so tantalizing. We think we are taking a break, or that in our own greatness we have planned a getaway and financed a trip to a wonderful place, believing that because of our amazing ideas that the grand experience is because of us. But, in reality, it is because of God. The unpleasant stuff we are escaping and think we are shedding is the "us" in all of this, and that sweet serenity that we seek, intuit, and become engrossed in is the "Him" of it all. Therefore, we think we have discovered something or brought something about when all along it is His beauty we sense—His peace that passes all understanding we have read about. Yet, there is something unexplainable about the ocean, the forests, and the meadows. I think it has a lot to do with the sounds. When you are around these places or in them, the only thing you hear is nature.

The ocean sound comes from below, out and away in a unique fashion, because as you stand before that incredible vastness, it's at your feet, evolving from beneath you and then pulling you in until together you merge away— out to the horizon. Its sound wells up and engulfs you as it spreads out before you. When you are there at the seashore, it is all you can hear, see, and smell. It blocks out your senses by crippling them into submission to only its offerings. The embellishments come from the sea birds, the foghorns, the crinkling of the sand beneath your feet and the negative ions that make you feel so positive that all is well.

The forest comes at you from all sides, above, before, and behind as it surrounds and engulfs you. Unlike the ocean, which is more distant, the forest draws you further in instead of taking you away. Its sound is in the trees that envelop you. It has the same dominance as the resonance of the surf exploring the rocks and beach. The wind whistles through the branches and it too comes and goes in waves augmented by the birds, the rustling limbs, branches, and the stillness of its core. Because of these wonders, it is no wonder that you get lost in its depths. You feel oddly safe in its mysterious majesty and it is truly a place of awesome splendor.

Meadows are tranquil; they are the calm and peaceful pleasure that grace quiet places. They exist to bring rest to your soul by the simple nature of their presence. When the morning winds sweep across their stillness, they become the adagio to God's symphony of creation. It is this song that lives forever in my heart. I have always said when God made meadows he had me in mind.

God bless us all,

—Ken Mansfield

ACKNOWLEDGMENTS

Philco is my alter author. We wrote these stories together. Each story is based on real events in my life and Philco has embellished each one with his fantastical imagination. We made this excursion into an alternate space called Hurricane Hills bonded together as one—maybe that is why people say I write like a Christian on acid. The beauty of Philco's interior quest led me to wonderful discoveries as I looked back at a gracious time gone by.

On this reflective trek I discovered I had developed deep friendships that began with my first book almost twenty years ago and these fellow wunderkinds of words have been traveling by my side up to the moment Philco got into that rusty old truck. So to my "Band of Brothers On The Run" Gabe Wicks, Bucky Rosenbaum, Dave Schroeder, Joel Miller and Brian Mitchell, I thank God for your friendship, encouragement, impartation of wisdoms deep and dear, for providing a safe place to rest between paragraphs and participles, great bar-b-que and fine wines. Thanks to fellow author and friend Marshall Terrill who also joined me many times along the writing way, adding and deleting words and ideas to many of my books.

Special Kudos to Bucky Rosenbaum, who was the first person to tell me I was an author and Brian Mitchell who has kept me going, kept me relative, and, most of all, kept me assured that what Bucky said was true as we floundered with my offerings in a sea of publisher rejections together. Thank you, Brian, and your great company Working Title Agency, for being a preposterously incredible literary agent and a solid true friend.

When Philco and I needed a friend to sit down with us to help weave and whittle our words to a point of clarity, Cara Highsmith offered her literary counsel, guidance, and incredible editing skills. As with Cara and all the people mentioned above I find it invigorating to be involved with people who are much more talented than I am.

As always, a tithe from proceeds of my books will go to founder and president Nancy Alcorn's fabulous ministry for young women: Mercy Multiplied. Check it out at mercymultiplied.com.

Most of all, I dedicate this to my wife, Connie, the light of my life and who from the first day we met has been the beginning and ending of all things eternal and lovely in our journey. She introduced me to the risen Lord...I love it that the first person I see every morning when I wake up is the one who saved my life.

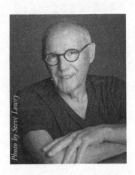

Photo by Steve Lowry

ABOUT THE AUTHOR

Ken Mansfield's legendary career in the music industry includes executive tenures as US Manager of Apple Records for The Beatles, Director at Capitol Records, Vice President at MGM Records, and President at Barnaby/CBS Records. As a record producer, he was instrumental in launching country music's "Outlaw" movement in the 1970s, producing Waylon Jennings' number-one 1975 landmark recording "Are You Ready for the Country" and Jessi Colter's number-one hit "I'm Not Lisa." Ken also produced the Gaither Vocal Band's 1991 GRAMMY and Dove Award-winning *Homecoming* album, which launched another historic movement, the resurgence of Southern gospel music via the Gaither Homecoming series of recordings, videos, and concerts. Ken is a published author of seven books.

*To contact or order autographed
books directly from Ken:*

MainMansfield.com

Bookings:

Premier Speakers Bureau,
Outreach Events, Ambassador Agency

By Philco